Going

American sprinting sensation Marion Jones has set her sights on winning a record five gold medals in track and field at the Olympic Games in Sydney. But whether she achieves that goal or not, she has already become known as one of the best athletes ever. Did you know . . .

. . . that Marion was the starting point guard for the national-champion University of North Carolina women's basketball team in her freshman year?

. . . that she went undefeated in races during 1998, winning 35 of the 36 track and field events she entered?

. . . that Marion speaks out about issues that are important to her in the "Mrs. Jones" Nike commercials? "Can you dig it?"

Read all about Marion's childhood dreams of being an Olympian, her struggle to overcome injuries and hardship, and her race to become the fastest woman in the world.

MARION JONES

THE FASTEST WOMAN IN THE WORLD

BILL GUTMAN

AN ARCHWAY PAPERBACK
Published by POCKET BOOKS

New York   London   Toronto   Sydney   Singapore

AN ARCHWAY PAPERBACK *Original*

An Archway Paperback published by
POCKET BOOKS, a division of Simon & Schuster, Inc.
1230 Avenue of the Americas, New York, NY 10020

Copyright © 2000 by Bill Gutman

ISBN: 0-7434-1876-X

First Archway Paperback printing September 2000

10 9 8 7 6 5 4 3 2 1

AN ARCHWAY PAPERBACK and colophon are registered
trademarks of Simon & Schuster, Inc.

Cover art by Rob Tringali Jr./Sports Chrome

Printed in the U.S.A.

IL 4+

Contents

Contents

MARION
JONES

Introduction

In the world of track and field, there have always been marquee events and a few special athletes who have captured the imagination of the public. Perhaps the most high-profile events have been two of the shortest—the 100-meter dash and the 200-meter dash. Both are speed races where the margin of victory can be measured in a hair's length, a hundredth of a second. For years, the man who wins the 100-meter dash in the Olympic Games or breaks a world record in the event has been called "the world's fastest human."

There is one thing that can bring a track athlete even more recognition and admiration than being the world's fastest human: combining speed with the ability to be a medal winner in more than one event. The grandest stage upon which to do this, of course, is the Olympics. The first athlete to achieve world-wide recognition for this feat was the legendary Jesse Owens. An African-American representing the United States in the politically charged atmosphere of Berlin, Germany, in 1936, Owens went about showing Nazi Party Chancellor Adolph Hitler there was no such thing as a superior master race.

Not only did Owens win the 100, he also won the 200, then was part of the winning United States 4 x 100 relay team, and finally showed his versatility by taking first place in the long jump. He won four gold medals in track and field in one Olympics, a feat some thought would never be duplicated. However, in 1984 another American, Carl Lewis, won the same four events at the Los Angeles Olympics. Though Lewis was also proclaimed the greatest track star of his time, his achievements were tarnished slightly by the fact that Soviet-bloc countries boycotted the Games and declined to participate. Nevertheless, Lewis caught the fancy of the public in much the same way Owens had nearly a half century earlier.

For many years, it was the men who usually had the star power when it came to track and field. Perhaps one reason was that American women didn't have the same success that the men had experienced in the sport. Things began changing somewhat at the 1960 Olympics in Rome when a twenty-year-old African-American named Wilma Rudolph won the 100 and the 200, then anchored the 4 x 100 relay team to victory. Rudolph, a polio victim as a youngster, won three gold medals and also became an instant sports icon. In a way, she opened the door for the women who followed.

It wasn't until the 1980s, however, that American women really began stepping up in the world of track and field. Suddenly, there was a whole group of new stars in the dashes—runners like Evelyn Ashford, Florence Griffith-Joyner, Gail Devers, and Gwen Torrence. Then there was Jackie Joyner-Kersee, proclaimed the best athlete of them all for her success in the grueling, seven-event heptathlon, as well as the long jump. All were stars with individual stories to tell.

In the long run, however, these great athletes may have to take a back seat to Marion Jones. Not only has Marion emerged, in the late 1990s, as one of the great sprinters of all time, she is also one of the premier athletes in the entire country, having been a collegiate basketball star at the University of North Carolina. While many of her fans and followers of the sport figured she would go from her Tar Heels hoop career right into the Women's National Basketball Association (WNBA), Marion did an about-face. She stopped her basketball career in its tracks and returned to her first love, the world of track and field.

Though she had been close to becoming a nationally ranked elite runner during her high school days in California, she more or less allowed the sport to take a back seat to her basketball career once she

3

reached college. When she returned, there was initially a question of whether she could regain the speed and the magic. Not only did she regain all of her skills, she began improving on them. Like her male predecessors, Marion showed she was one of the world's best long jumpers as well as the premier sprinter at 100 and 200 meters—the world's fastest human on the ladies' side.

With the 2000 Olympic Games scheduled to be held in Sydney, Australia, Marion Jones is intent upon making history. She has announced that she will try to win an unprecedented five gold medals—in the 100-and 200-meter dashes, the long jump, and as part of the 4 x 100 and 4 x 400-meter relay teams. To those familiar with track and field, that represents a daunting task. For those who know Marion Jones, however, it is an ambition that could well be within reach. She is an athlete whose determination matches her natural abilities, and whose desire to win and excel is perhaps second to none.

In an Olympic year, some feel that Marion has put too much pressure on herself and too much stress on her body. Sprinters are finely tuned athletes who must make sudden and explosive movements, exposing themselves to pulled muscles and other track-related injuries. Marion not only sprints, but long jumps and runs the longer, 400-meter distance. In addition, competing in at least three events in most major meets is taxing, with preliminary heats and jumps, followed by pressure-packed finals. Marion has already had her share of injuries, in both basketball and track, including her well-publicized back spasms at the 1999 World Track and Field Championships.

So the pressure builds. Can Marion Jones make track history? As she continues her quest, more people are learning about this remarkable woman with incredible athletic skills and dogged determination. She could well become the first major athletic story of the new millennium.

Chapter 1
A Star Is Born

No one can predict athletic stardom from day one. First, the genes have to be there, the natural talent that will blossom as a young boy or girl grows and begins to play sports. Then there has to be opportunity—to be encouraged to play and learn the skills, to find the competition, to acquire a good, understanding coach, and finally to acquire a love of the sporting life. However, that still doesn't ensure that an athlete will continue to progress and star at each new level as he or she becomes older.

Once again there has to be a support group—family, coaches, friends—who continue to encourage a young athlete in the right way, not forcing or pushing too hard, but letting the pieces fall into place naturally. Yet that still doesn't guarantee reaching the top. All things being equal, the final push has to come from the athlete. He or she has to develop character, an inner drive to excel, and a will to win that refuses to yield, refuses to be defeated. Only when all these factors are in place will a world-class athlete emerge.

When Marion Jones was born on October 12, 1975, in Los Angeles, the odds of her becoming a future star seemed long, indeed. Her mother, also named Marion, had spent her early years in Belize, which was then known as British Honduras. Her grandmother, Eva Hulse, died at the age of forty-three, with her grandfather, George, promising his wife that he would see their daughter, Marion, and her brother make it through high school.

There was no free education in Belize at the time, so George Hulse moved to Guatemala to try to earn a better living and send money back for the children. It was a tough life, with Marion Hulse being raised by distant relatives who became her guardians. She received her education, though, eventually spending two years at a secretarial school in London. Then she came to the United States in 1968 and spent two years in New York before moving to Los Angeles.

In New York, she had a very brief marriage to a man named Albert Kelly, some twenty years her senior. They had a son, also named Albert, then went their separate ways. After she moved to Los Angeles, Marion Kelly met a man named George Jones. They were soon married, but again there were problems. Jones would leave her, then return, doing this several times. By the time young Marion was born, the marriage was coming apart. Jones finally left for good and the couple divorced.

Fortunately, Marion's mother had a good job as a legal secretary, and the lawyers she worked for helped her sort things out during and after the divorce. She was determined to raise her children well and give them a good life. One of young Marion's earliest memories was sitting in the living room of her home in 1981, watching the wedding of Britain's Prince Charles to Princess Diana. She was not yet six years old when she turned to her mother and said:

"They have a red carpet to walk on, because they're special people. When will they roll out a red carpet for me?"

There wouldn't be a red carpet right away, but there was always sports. Young Marion grew quickly and began following her half brother, Albert, onto the streets and playgrounds, where he engaged in a myriad of sports and outdoor activities. Even when she was just six years old, Marion was already doing the things brother Albert was doing.

"She could dribble a basketball, run races, throw and hit a baseball, and compete with my friends and me," Albert said. "When it came to playing games, it was almost like having a brother."

By the time she was in kindergarten and first grade, she was the tallest girl in the class, already too fast and strong for the other kids to compete with her. Maybe that was step one to becoming a great athlete, but there was still so much ahead of her. Life changed somewhat in 1983 when her mother married a retired postal worker named Ira Tolar and the family moved to Palmdale, a small desert city fifty miles north of Los Angeles. Marion Tolar continued to work as a legal secretary while Ira stayed at home and took young Marion under his wing. He was as much of a father as she would ever have.

"Whenever he went somewhere, whether it was to the store or to the lodge to hang out with his buddies, I'd be right there," Marion said, in later years. "It was almost as if I was living in his back pocket."

During the next few years Marion grew taller and stronger, and began to excel even more as an athlete. Because she was already so good at everything, she often played with and against boys, rather than girls. She was so good in Little League that many parents watching in the stands, and seeing this young girl dominate the game, called out for the opposing pitcher to bean her with the baseball. It got so bad that her mother took her out of Little League and enrolled her in a gymnastics class instead. That was, in effect, the end of her organized baseball career.

Fortunately, it wasn't the same with other sports. She continued to play with her brother and his friends, though they were four and five years older than she was. "She was strong, almost as tall as most of my friends, and she never, ever quit," Albert said. There was something else that Marion soon realized from playing sports all the time. Playing and excelling was one thing, but nothing was quite as satisfying as winning. She loved being on the winning team, or crossing the finish line first in a race, or being honored with a medal or ribbon for her athletic achievements. The desire, or need, to win and finish first made her work even harder. She practiced the basic skills of basketball and gymnastics for hours on end. Sometimes her mother or stepfather would have go out to find her and order her inside. She was not living the life of a typical little girl.

"I had no use for dolls or any girl things," Marion would say. "I didn't even have any girlfriends."

Life for Marion and her family took a cruel turn just a few short years later. In 1987, Ira Tolar suffered a stroke and died. His loss would be felt by the entire family and especially by Marion, since he was the only father figure she had ever known. As her half brother Albert said, "Ira was always there for my sister. He talked to her, answered her questions, helped her with her homework, took her to tee-ball games. Then he was gone."

For Marion, it was a great loss. Ira Tolar had filled a void in her life and undoubtedly would have continued to do so had he lived. Yet like so many youngsters who don't live with both parents, Marion had a yearning that would never really go away. As she would say years later, "I loved Ira to death, but he was not my real dad."

At the time of Ira Tolar's death, Marion's half

brother Albert was in Belize with an uncle, so Marion and her mother were left alone. Marion's nickname on the street was "Hard Nails," for her toughness and spunk. Her mother knew she would have a tough job ahead of her because she already felt her daughter was destined for something special. She knew that if she raised her own daughter the way she had been raised, she would risk losing her.

"She was the type of child who would say, 'If I don't get this or that, I'm going to jump off this ledge,'" Marion Tolar said. "If I said, 'Go ahead, jump,' she would have. I knew that she would defy me, test me, and there were many rebellions. But I decided that she was special, that I had to find a way to nurture these qualities, not beat them out of her."

After that, Marion Tolar began to plan the family's life to ensure her daughter's success and happiness. It wasn't always easy, but she was right about one thing. Marion Jones was indeed special, and she would soon begin showing it to all who watched her perform.

Chapter 2

The First Glimpse of Greatness

Even before Marion Jones entered junior high school there were flashes of athletic brilliance. Much of it was born out of her grit and determination to succeed. When her mother had taken her out of Little League and enrolled her in a gymnastics class, Marion knew virtually nothing of the new sport. One of the first things she saw was the older girls doing maneuvers such as cartwheels, back flips, and handstands. She asked the instructor immediately to show her how to do them.

Within a month, the young Marion had a skill level equal to most of the older girls who had been practicing for years. Then, she passed them and was doing the maneuvers nearly as well as the instructor. This was a quality that would never leave her. Show her something athletically, and she would practice until she not only mastered the new skill, but had conquered it completely, to the point where she was outstanding.

Knowing her daughter needed topflight programs and competition, Marion Tolar moved once again. This time she took the family from Palmdale southwest to the suburban Los Angeles town of Sherman Oaks, so that Marion could attend Pinecrest Junior High. There, Marion began to excel at both track and basketball. By 1989, when she was in the eighth grade, she ran bests of 12.01 for 100 meters, 24.06 for 200 meters, and 56.73 for 400 meters. The times were incredible since Marion was just thirteen years old.

Marion Tolar, realizing that her daughter was, indeed, a special athlete, once again moved the family. This time she went to the Ventura County town of Camarillo, so that young Marion could attend Rio Mesa High School. Rio Mesa had a star sprinter that year, a girl named Angela Burnham. She won prep Athlete of the Year honors in 1989 as a senior, with times of 11.52 in the 100 and 23.49 in the 200. Brian Fitzgerald, the track coach at Rio Mesa, couldn't say enough good things about Burnham. But one day, when he was speaking again about his start sprinter, Fitzgerald surprised everyone by saying,

"We have another kid coming up who's going to be even better."

That other kid was Marion. She began at Rio Mesa in the fall of 1989. Before she could show her stuff on the track (a spring sport), she went out for the basketball team, the hoop season beginning in the late fall. Al Walker, the Rio Mesa girls' basketball coach, couldn't help but notice the speed and the spring in the legs of the fourteen-year-old freshman. During practice one day, he asked her on a whim whether she could jump up and touch the bottom of the backboard.

Marion, who was already close to her full height of five feet ten inches, jumped up and easily slapped the backboard. Intrigued, Walker decided to challenge the freshman again. He asked her if she could touch the rim. A basketball rim is ten feet off the floor. Girls, as a rule, cannot jump as high as boys and very few, even in the WNBA, can dunk the ball. Now, Coach Walker was asking a fourteen-year-old girl if she could touch the rim. Not one to back away from any challenge, Marion ran in from the top of the circle, jumped, and amazed everyone who was watching.

"She not only touched the rim," Coach Walker recalled, "she grabbed it. She was well above the basket. I just turned to my assistant and said, 'Did you see that?'"

After that, Walker used to kid with Marion about the possibility of her becoming the first high school girl to dunk the ball during a game. She would always shake her head, saying she didn't think she could. Then the coach would tell her that if she did, it had better be in a game the team was going to win, because he would get up from the bench, go outside, pay his way in, and watch the rest of the game from the stands. Marion didn't dunk, but that was probably the only thing she didn't do in a high school game.

Needless to say, she was a starter from day one and quickly had her average up above the 20 point-per-game mark. Her coach and teammates also saw the great intensity she had and her ability to focus on the business at hand. Before each game she would become quiet and just stare straight ahead, looking at nothing in particular. She was obviously in a deep concentration, visualizing the game and what she would have to do. Her coach called it the look of an assassin.

When her first high school season ended, Marion Jones had already made her mark as a future big-time basketball star. She averaged 24.5 points and grabbed more than 11 rebounds a game. More than that, she was a leader on the floor and a player who simply hated to lose. Winning was more important to her than individual achievements. If she scored 50 points but her team lost, she was unhappy. Miserable, in fact. Basketball was a team game. You could play great and still lose. Track was a different story. Whether you won or lost in an individual race was entirely up to you.

Once track started, Marion pursued it with the same intensity and zeal that had been her trademark during the basketball season. It was as if she was getting better by the day. Not only did she have personal bests of 11.62 in the 100, 23.70 in the 200, and 54.21 in the 400, but she also won both the 100- and 200-meter championships at the California High School

State meet. As just a freshman at Rio Mesa High, Marion Jones had become a superstar in two sports, an athlete who seemed destined to make her mark in a very big way in upcoming years. She had all the qualities needed for greatness, including the inner strength and determination that said, *I will not lose.*

Now sports were not only dominating Marion's life, but her mother's, as well. Marion Tolar knew how much her daughter loved to play, noticing how young Marion's eyes would light up when she was going to a track meet or a basketball game. So her mother was always looking for a better situation, for ways to ensure that her daughter would have the best possible chance to continue and make her mark.

Her sophomore year at Rio Mesa was more of the same. She excelled at basketball for a second straight season, then burned up the track in the spring. Not only did she repeat her victories in the California High School State meet, she also won the 100- and 200-meter dashes at the USA Juniors meet, and was named High School Athlete of the Year. What's more, her personal bests in the 100 (11.17) and 200 (22.76) were now world-class times. At the end of the season the *Track & Field News* ranked her tenth best in the country in the 100 and fifth best in the 200. All that at fifteen years of age!

That still wasn't all. Marion's times in the 100 and 200 were good enough to qualify her for the United States Track and Field Championships, which were held that summer at Randall's Island in New York

City. At age fifteen, Marion Jones was about to compete against the best runners in the world. Instead of being overtaken by nerves, she found herself strangely calm as she lined up for the start of the 100.

"I remember lining up in the blocks," she said. "I looked to my right and saw Evelyn Ashford, then looked to my left and saw Gwen Torrence. I had some butterflies earlier, but when I got into the blocks I felt focused and calm."

She would finish sixth in the 100, then run to a surprising fourth-place finish in the 200. Had she managed a third in the 200 she would have qualified for a place on the United States team that went to the World Championships in Tokyo that year. At age fifteen, she was already a world-class runner and very close to being among the best.

"I saw how fast I had run and how fast they had run," Marion said, "and I knew I could be right with them. I knew it wouldn't be long."

That summer, Marion was attending a weekend basketball camp run by a man named Mel Sims. He was a well-respected coach in the Pasadena area who sometimes took all-star teams on good will visits to the Far East. In the summer of 1991, Sims planned a trip to Hong Kong and China, his all-star team slated to play against high school teams in those two Asian countries. The problem was that each athlete had to pay $2,500 to go on the trip. To give her daughter what she felt would be a great experience,

Marion Tolar worked an extra job and managed to put the money together.

Marion enjoyed the trip immensely. In Shenzhen, China, she amazed the crowd on a fast break by catching a high pass in midair as she was leaping out-of-bounds. Before coming down, she flipped the ball over her head to a teammate, then quickly came back in bounds, took a return pass, and scored. The crowd went wild, as did her teammates.

"It was one of those three or four plays you see in your life that you always remember," Coach Sims said.

When the public-address announcer asked the coach about Marion, he explained that she was not only the number one basketball player in the state of California, but the number one track star, as well, a state champion. The announcer then relayed the information to the crowd, perhaps making her achievements sound even greater in translation and they cheered for a full ten minutes. The game actually had to be stopped while the crowd roared. After that, people began coming up to her on the street, asking for an autograph or simply to shake her hand. She was already becoming an international star.

"Little kids would come up to us on the street," Marion said. "They had never seen black people before in their lives and many of them rubbed our skin to see if the color would come off. But we really had a ball."

Back in California, Marion still had two more

years of high school. Again, however, circumstances dictated a change. Marion Tolar was about to move her family once more and, as usual, the reason was to further her daughter's growing sports career. Not that there was anything inherently wrong with Rio Mesa High. In fact, Marion was very happy at the racially and ethnically mixed high school, which had almost equal proportions of whites, blacks, and Latinos. Marion had many friends there, and their presence often deflected some of the pressures of big-time sports, which were beginning to build. In fact, basketball coach Walker had an expression. He said that Marion's full-throttle pursuit of athletic excellence often took away her chances to be a "full-on kid."

The summer after her sophomore year, Marion met and began working out with Elliott Mason, who was a psychologist and counselor at Los Angeles Harbor College. He had also been Olympic champion Evelyn Ashford's running partner. Mason impressed Marion's mother because he quickly showed his first concern was for the young athlete's health. He sent Marion to an orthopedist to see if she had stopped growing, just to make sure the strenuous workouts wouldn't damage her joints. Because Mason seemed interested in Marion as a person first and an athlete second, her mother wanted very much for him to keep working with her.

Her track coach at Rio Mesa, Brian Fitzgerald, could only work with her during the track season, so it was Elliott Mason who drove a long way to supervise her workouts before school began. Both Marion and her mother were thinking about the 1992 Olympic trials already and they felt she needed additional coaching. So they asked Coach Fitzgerald if Mason could attend practices, watch Marion, make some suggestions, and perhaps put her through some private drills. However, the arrangement couldn't be made.

Now Marion Tolar knew she had to make another decision. After making some inquiries she decided to move once more. This time Marion would be attending Thousand Oaks High, which was in an upscale district economically and almost totally white. All things being equal, Marion admitted she would have preferred to remain at Rio Mesa.

"I had gotten used to my friends at Rio Mesa and the transition didn't go very well," she said. "Besides my teammates, I didn't feel really comfortable with many of the students at Thousand Oaks. It was never a racial thing. It was more economic, I guess."

As far as sports were concerned, however, it was a different story. Art Green, the track coach at Thousand Oaks, said he would have no problem working with Elliott Mason and he simply added him to his coaching staff. The two coaches worked very well together and, as a tandem, made Marion an even better runner, not to mention giving the school one of the best track teams in the state.

It was the same with basketball. Marion didn't

have that much support on the hardwood at Rio Mesa, but the team she joined at Thousand Oaks was already one of the best in the state. Charles Brown was a veteran coach in his mid-fifties who treated Marion like every other player. If she made a mistake in practice, he made her run laps, no questions asked. He had a no-nonsense, tough approach to the game, which Marion respected. She liked Coach Brown and, more importantly, she trusted him.

Another reason the change worked out so well was Marion's attitude. She didn't come in as if she was going to take over the team. Thousand Oaks had a star point guard named Michelle Palmisano and Coach Brown was concerned that the two might vie for the leadership role. Because Marion was the team's tallest player at five feet ten inches, she played underneath the basket or out on the wing. The two players assumed coleadership roles and worked beautifully together.

Marion and her Thousand Oaks teammates got off to a good start in the 1991–92 season. Not surprisingly, Marion was living up to all her advance notices, making Coach Brown, her teammates, the rest of the students and fans happy she had transferred to their school. Then, midway through the season, disaster struck. Thousand Oaks was playing at Simi Valley and Marion was defending down near her own hoop. She tipped a pass away, grabbed the loose ball, and raced upcourt. Even then, Marion was probably one of, if not the fastest player in the country going end to end, with or without the ball.

As she neared the hoop she was moving full tilt and a Simi Valley player moved over to try to block her path to the basket. Maybe it was Marion's speed that frightened her. Instead of trying to go for the block, or simply standing still to take a charge, the defender suddenly ducked, covered her head, and turned her back to Marion. There was no way Marion could avoid the collision. Her knee hit first and then she went into a somersault before hitting the court . . . hard.

She had put out her arm instinctively to break the fall. Instead, she broke her wrist in two places, then hit her chin and dislocated her jaw. It was a frightening injury because while she realized her wrist was probably broken, she couldn't understand why she couldn't move her mouth and couldn't talk. It was also the first serious injury of her career.

"At the hospital it took them a dozen tries to set my wrist," Marion recalled. "I remember screaming in pain. Then in the X-ray room they began moving it around as if nothing was wrong. I told them I had a broken wrist and had to ask them to take it easy."

The ensuing weeks were very difficult, as well. All athletes face the possibility of injury every time they compete, but it never gets easier for the simple reason that an athlete who can't compete is like a fish without water. For Marion, this one was especially difficult because it was the first major one. She became depressed and, while her mother tried to help her all she could, the two were often at odds, snapping at each other.

"Marion was miserable," her mother said. "I stopped working, stayed home to nurse her, cook for her, help her get around, but still felt I couldn't do anything for her. She just didn't want me to."

The injury brought another question about Marion's pursuit of two sports to the forefront. Here she was, playing high school basketball, which kept her from reporting to track until the season was over. So basketball would be cutting into a track season that would culminate with the Olympic trials in the summer of 1992. Now she was injured and there was no telling how it would affect the coming track season. Yet Art Green, the coach of the Thousand Oaks track team, wouldn't add fuel to the fire.

"I've never told any kid to give up another sport for my sport," the coach said. "I don't think anybody has the right to do that. Besides, I love watching [Marion] play basketball."

Others, however, felt that for an athlete expected to excel, and one approaching world-class while still in high school, the pressures might be too great, with burnout becoming a real possibility. Many high school athletes, pushed by parents, pressured by coaches and teammates, suddenly seem to lose sight of the fact that sports should be fun. Soon, they find themselves looking for other outlets. Many of them abandon sports completely, their careers over before they begin.

That wasn't the case, however, with Marion. As ferocious a competitor as she was, she still loved to compete, loved to win, loved to challenge herself to do better. She also loved both sports—basketball and track—and seemed to know that playing both was the right thing for her to do at the time.

"People used to say to me back then, 'Why don't you decide?'" she recalled. "But the way I saw it, there was no need for me to make a decision then. I knew that sooner or later I wouldn't be able to continue both sports at the same time, but I also wanted to be able to say I did what I wanted to do. I wanted to be able to say I was happy."

Marion's wrist was in a cast for six weeks. Finally, she was the one who insisted the doctor remove it. He then wrapped the wrist in a brace and warned her to take it easy. Knowing her body, she rejoined the basketball team almost immediately. Though she had missed a good chunk of the season, her game was as good as ever. Playing in a tournament game that year, she scored 30 points, grabbed 19 rebounds, and blocked 9 shots in an incredible display of her tremendous talent. Despite the injury, she was named all-county and all-state. Once the season ended, she quickly reported to the track team. Within a few months, the entire track world would know just how good Marion Jones had become.

Chapter 3
Big Decisions

By this time, Marion was a tall and graceful athlete with polished skills that made her appear to move effortlessly, whether it be on the track or basketball court. She had a pleasant, pretty face with soft features and a ready smile, a look that belied her inner toughness and determination to always finish on top. Make no mistake about it, though, Marion Jones was already considered a world-class athlete on the track and a basketball player with the skills and temperament to join an elite collegiate program and eventually the WNBA. Some time very soon, however, Marion, her mother, and her coaches knew that some big decisions would have to be made.

Her wrist healed, she took up right where she left off on the track—winning her races with an explosiveness only seen with the top performers in the sport. She had new personal bests in the 100 (11.14) and 200 (22.58) while winning both events at the California High School State meet for the third year in a row. Once again she was named High School Athlete of the Year, and won both sprint events at the USA junior meet, her 200 time of 22.58 setting an American junior record. At the end of the season she was ranked fifth in the United States in both the 100 and 200 by the *Track and Field News*. Only in 1992, the end of her high school season didn't signal the end of track. There was still another event coming up, one that had increasing meaning for Marion Jones.

The 1992 Olympic Games were scheduled to be held in Barcelona, Spain, in late summer, with the United States Olympic trials slated for New Orleans. Though she was still just sixteen years old, Marion decided to go for it. Marion had been acutely aware of the Olympics since 1984, when she was just eight years old. That was the year the Games were held in Los Angeles and Carl Lewis duplicated Jesse Owens's feat of winning four gold medals. After watching the Games on television, young Marion went to her room and wrote on her blackboard:

I want to be an Olympic champion.

Marion would say later that she loved watching the Games on television, noticing the competition between the athletes and the joy they showed when they crossed the finish line first and accepted their gold medals. "The whole Olympic spirit was just so exciting to me," she added.

She especially noticed the women athletes in 1984, as women's sports continued to grow and come into their own. There was Evelyn Ashford and Jackie Joyner-Kersee, Joan Benoit, and Mary Lou Retton—all excelling in their respective events and touching a chord in young Marion. Then came 1988, when the Olympics moved on to Seoul, Korea. By this time, Marion was on the brink of high school and ready to start her own track career, so it was no surprise she was captivated by Florence Griffth-Joyner, the incomparable Flo-Jo.

Flo-Jo was a beautiful woman, stylish with flowing hair, long painted fingernails, and colorful tracksuits. When she matched her style with substance, she took the track world by storm. At the Olympic trials in Indianapolis, Griffith-Joyner exploded out of the blocks and won the 100-meter dash in a world record time of 10.49, setting a standard that has not been broken to this day. She also won the 200 qualifying run. Then, at the Olympics, she won her double, taking the 100 and then setting another world record of 21.34 in the 200. That mark, too, remains the sport's standard for women at that distance. She was the star of the games and made yet another impression on young Marion Jones.

"I don't think I fully grasped how fast she had run," Marion said. "I knew she looked like she was flying, that her feet never really hit the ground."

So it was no surprise when Marion made an Olympic championship one of her athletic goals. For a track and field performer, Olympic gold is the pinnacle, the ultimate achievement, something to be remembered and savored for a lifetime. With Elliott Mason still coaching her, Marion joined other Olympic hopefuls in New Orleans, where she would run both the 100 and 200. The summer heat was intense during the trials, not optimum conditions, and while Marion didn't perform a miracle, she acquitted herself extremely well, especially for a sixteen year-old with limited world-class experience.

In the 200, she ran a great race, her long strides making up ground in the final yards. In the world of track and field, a microsecond can mean the difference between first and second or, in Marion's case, third and fourth. Her time was 22.58 seconds, which went into the books as a national high school record that still stands today. Unfortunately, the third place finisher ran a 22.51. Marion was fourth by a scant, seven one-hundredths (.07) of a second. Only the top three go on to the Olympics, so Marion barely missed.

Then came the 100. Marion wasn't yet quite there, finishing in sixth place. While that was a bit disappointing, there was a consolation prize. She had earned a spot as an alternate on the 4 x 100 relay team. Alternates sometimes run in the early heats, saving the top runners for the semifinals and finals. However, there is also a chance that the alternates might not run at all. Yet if the 4 x 100 team won a medal, the alternates would receive one as well. It was a chance for her to go to the Olympics at age sixteen. It seemed a no brainer. But, then again, Marion Jones was no ordinary athlete. She thought about it, talked to her mother and her coach . . . and turned the offer down!

"I wanted to *earn* a gold medal," she said, "work and sweat for it. Years from now, when I show people my gold medals, I want to be able to say I ran for them."

It was a tough decision and, in many ways, a courageous one. Some of her friends and teammates thought she was crazy to pass up a chance to go to the Olympics, enjoy the atmosphere, possibly run in the heats and win a medal. Just being there, many felt, would better prepare her for the 1996 Olympic Games, which would be held in Atlanta, Georgia. Marion, however, had made her choice. It was final. She would have one more year of high school, then go off to college, keep working, and prepare herself for Atlanta. Barcelona was out.

Unfortunately, it would not be business as usual in 1993. Marion ran into a crisis, not of her own making, that threatened to curtail, maybe even destroy, her track career. She was a senior at Thousand Oaks that year, getting ready for her final season of basketball before moving onto track once more. By this time, her track career had come under the auspices of the Athletics Congress (TAC), which was the sport's governing body, an organization that would soon change its name to USA Track & Field Federation. At any rate, once an athlete competed at the international level, he or she was subject to random drug testing. The TAC would send letters to randomly selected athletes, directing them to report for a drug testing site in forty-eight hours. Marion was sent such a letter that September.

At that time, her mother had arranged to have all mail from the TAC forwarded to Elliott Mason's office at Harbor College. That way, she felt, an important letter wouldn't be lying outside her door all day while she was at work. Unfortunately, the letter requesting a drug test for Marion was somehow tossed aside in the mail room of the college. When it finally reached Mason's desk, it was too late. Marion received another letter from the TAC. This one said she was suspended for four years!

"Elliott called them as soon as he found the letter," Marion's mother said, "but they didn't want to hear it. In their eyes, Marion had committed a crime and had to be punished. They were going to make an example of her."

The way the TAC looked at it, if an athlete didn't report for a drug test, it was tantamount to an admission of guilt. The athlete didn't report because he or she couldn't pass. To make matters worse, Marion learned of her suspension by reading it in the papers. She knew other people would read it and assume she was guilty of using an illegal or banned drug.

"I'm in high school, beating everybody, and I'm on cloud nine," she said, "and all of a sudden I read I'm suspended for four years. I didn't know what to do."

The suspension didn't cover her high school meets, only open and international competition. But this was her last year of high school and while she could go on to compete at the college level, four years away from international competition would seriously compromise her career. It was a matter of a freak accident, a misplaced letter. Otherwise, Marion would have gladly complied with the test. TAC was simply following their rules to the letter. Marion and her mother hired a lawyer, but it did no good. Then they brought the renowned attorney Johnnie Cochran into the fray.

Cochran would gain notoriety of another kind a short time later when he was part of the O. J. Simpson defense team. Now he heard about the Marion Jones case from his wife, who was Elliott Mason's cousin. With all the kids who were getting into real trouble on the streets, he felt it was worth going to war for the reputation of a young woman whose life and achievements had been nothing short of amazing. He took the case and forfeited his fee.

Because they knew a simple appeal would be fruitless, Cochran and his associates took another approach. First, they pointed out that the letter directing Marion to report did not contain Elliott Mason's room number at Harbor College. They also questioned the arbitrary way the suspension process was handled. Finally, Cochran gave the TAC one more thing to think about.

"I told them I was going to federal court if the suspension wasn't overturned," he explained. "We would have won, too, and we would have knocked them out of everything they were doing [with the drug testing]."

Within days, Marion's suspension was overturned. One reason was thought to be good old-fashioned timing. Many members of TAC felt the system had become unfair and were looking for ways to change it. Shortly after Marion was reinstated, the system was modified and a phone number was set up so that athletes could call to see if they were scheduled to report for testing.

As for Marion, she could now relax and continue to compete. The 1993 season saw her add another event to her already impressive repertoire. During her junior year she had occasionally practiced some other events, such as the hurdles. That, however, simply didn't work out. Then she began to think about the long jump. She knew that Carl Lewis, one of her idols, had successfully competed in the sprints and long jump, as had Jesse Owens years earlier. She also admired Jackie Joyner-Kersee, who competed in the long jump as an individual event while concentrating on the difficult heptathlon.

Finally, with Coach Green's blessing, she began to compete in the long jump during her senior year. Without knowing the mechanics of the event, she was already jumping in the 19-foot range. Her first competition at California Polytechnic State University produced a winning jump of 19'10", and that represented the best jump in the nation by a high school girl to that point in the season. Marion had found yet another event, though she knew she still needed to work hard at it.

"I didn't know what I was doing," she said, after that first victory. "I really wasn't thinking about technique, just about winning and how far I could jump."

Perhaps her problems with the TAC over the drug-testing fiasco derailed her a bit. At season's end she went to the state meet and once again won both the 100- and 200-meter dashes, though for the first time her winning times were slower than the previous year. Then, however, she added yet another title by winning the long jump with a leap of 22 feet, one-half inch, just short of a national high school record that had been standing for thirteen years. In four years, she had won nine championships at the California State Meet and was honored by being asked to take a victory lap.

Marion ran the track slowly, waving to the crowd of 12,000, who collectively rose to their feet and cheered. Though she didn't know it at the time, Marion's victory lap was the only one ever taken by a competitor at the California State Meet, which had been held every year since 1915. That's how special Marion Jones had been.

She was no less successful in basketball. During

her two years at Thousand Oaks, she led the team to the California Interscholastic Foundation (CIF) Division I championship game each year, the team winning it in 1992. As a senior, she averaged 22.8 points a game, and was named CIF Player of the Year and the Most Valuable Player (MVP) of Ventura County.

So now there were more decisions to be made. She not only had to pick a college, but had to decide whether to again pursue two sports, or to concentrate on just one. With so many colleges aware of her athletic prowess, everyone had something to say and suggestions of what would be best for her. But, as always, the ultimate decision on Marion Jones's future had to come from Marion Jones.

Chapter 4

In the Tar Heel Tradition

Marion had never been a secret to the colleges, not from the moment she burst onto the sports scene as a freshman at Rio Mesa High. Major universities with big time athletic programs make it their business to know about the top high school stars. They watch them, scout them, screen them, evaluate them and, if they feel the athletes can contribute to their institution, they recruit them. While most top athletes don't begin hearing from colleges until they are juniors or seniors, Marion received her first recruiting letter just a week after she began high school.

That one was from Arizona State University and it was just the tip of the iceberg. During the entire length of her high school career the letters continued to come. The majority of the letters were recruiting her for track. While she was certainly a great basketball player, maybe one of the best, there were still plenty of other players colleges could pursue. But as a track star who still had not reached her peak, she was perceived as the absolute best.

Many of the letters told her flat out that it would be in her worst interests to play college basketball. "They said my future was in track," Marion explained.

That kind of thinking, however, didn't always sit well with Marion. She never liked it when others told her about her best interests. Some of the recruiters realized this and felt it was best for everyone concerned if they offered Marion the opportunity to play both sports. Schools that wanted her as a basketball player as well as a track performer also realized that she would probably sit out the 1996 basketball season while she prepared to try out for the United States Olympic team.

One school that did it the right way was the University of North Carolina. When North Carolina recruited Marion, she was visited by assistant coaches from both the basketball and track teams together. That alone didn't guarantee anything. Marion's mother was also looking for colleges that had a good record of graduating minority students who played varsity sports. They also checked out the journalism programs at the schools since Marion wanted to make that her major. Finally, the two narrowed it down to three schools—the University of Florida, Ohio State University, and University of North Carolina.

Marion at first favored Florida, while her mother seemed to prefer North Carolina. However, she never visited the Gainesville, Florida, campus. A trip to Chapel Hill, home of UNC, changed everything. Marion liked the campus, met professors and members of the basketball team, and learned about the journalism school, which was considered one of the best. She also liked the friendliness of the people.

"I was blown back by having people walk by and say good morning, people who didn't even know you," she said. "Coming from California, where everybody kept to themselves, I knew this was where I wanted to go to school."

In the fall of 1993, Marion left California for Chapel Hill. Her mother, feeling that families should stick together, moved east with her. It wouldn't always be an easy situation.

Marion put it this way. "I had always been independent, but when I went to college, that was multiplied ten times. My mother and I butted heads, a lot."

As for her mother, Marion Tolar made it sound simple. "I wasn't trying to control her. I just wanted to watch her play ball."

Fortunately, it wouldn't be a major problem, just a case of a mother and daughter being a bit too close during the daughter's college years. But the two would eventually work it out. The important thing was that Marion was about to embark on the next phase of her life. She was joining a team that had a tremendous basketball tradition. The majority of that tradition, however, was on the men's side. Coached by the legendary Dean Smith, the Tar Heels were a perennial national power. The men had won three national championships, the first in 1957 when Frank McGuire coached the team to a title game victory over Wilt Chamberlain and Kansas University.

Smith's North Carolina teams had won in 1982, when a freshman named Michael Jordan made a last-second jump shot against Georgetown University, and again in 1993, the year before Marion arrived. Jordan was the best of many Carolina All-Americans, a host of whom went on to play in the National Basketball Association (NBA). Though the women's program didn't have the long history of success, there were signs that it was coming alive. A 23-7 season under Coach Sylvia Hatchell in 1992–93 augured good things. There were a number of fine players returning from that season and now they had Marion Jones.

Of course, there were questions. Many of them centered on just how Marion planned to split her time between two sports. Her scholarship was primarily for basketball, with allowances for her to run some track. "I love track, and I wanted to keep it like that," she said. "So many young runners get burned out. I figured I do both, but in the beginning, I needed discipline, and the Carolina basketball program was very structured."

Honest as always, Marion joined the team at the

beginning of practice and immediately showed everyone what a great talent she was. In fact, it was her tremendous natural talent that presented Coach Hatchell with an incipient problem. Where was she going to play her freshman star? Because Marion was one of the tallest girls on her high school teams, she almost always played close to the basket or out on the wing where she could cut to the hoop and score from in close. Thus her experience handling the ball and setting up teammates with passes was somewhat limited.

However, the Lady Tar Heels had three solid frontcourt players returning—Sylvia Crawley, Tonya Sampson, and Charlotte Smith—and Coach Hatchell couldn't see benching one of the three. Looking to put the strongest team on the floor, she began toying with the idea of giving Marion the ball and letting her run the team. When the coach told Marion of her plan to convert her into a point guard, the freshman wasn't sure it was such a good idea. But the coach didn't waver. She felt a talent like Marion could make the change quickly and effectively. The more she saw in the ensuing weeks, the more she felt she had made the right decision.

"Marion has a focus on what she wants to do like no one I've ever seen," the coach said. "She lets no one and nothing interfere. And she's so coachable. She'd watch films, ask questions. Whatever you showed her, she would perfect it. She was like a sponge."

The team continued working toward the upcoming season with Marion learning more about the point guard position every day. She worked on her ballhandling, passing, and court vision, which could be distinctly different in the backcourt than when she played up front. She was also toughening up for the rigors of big-time college basketball. Coach Hatchell had all her players working with weights, something Marion hadn't done much of before. Soon she could press more than two hundred pounds and was gaining muscular weight.

In addition, the Lady Tar Heels held unofficial practice sessions with the men's team, and Marion had the pleasure of playing against the likes of Jerry Stackhouse and Rasheed Wallace, a pair of All-Americans who would go on to star in the NBA.

"The men would push us around a bit," Marion said. "A lot of coaches don't like their women playing against the guys because it's too rough, but I think that helped us. We had some heated games."

As soon as she had that early taste of the collegiate game, Marion knew she had made the right decision. Now she was playing alongside women who were skilled and competitive, and who loved everything about the game. Even when practice was over, they played some more, organizing pickup games whenever they had the chance. Marion described that first taste of collegiate ball in three simple words.

"It was wonderful," she said.

Despite a fine season the year before, the returning players were still smarting from a 74–54 loss to Tennessee in the National Collegiate Athletic Association (NCAA) tournament, a defeat viewed as embarrassing to all of them. Starting with the first practice of the season, Coach Hatchell had the team come to the center of the court, grasp hands, and yell "National Champions!" They did it each day, making their goal a recurring theme so no one would forget it, not for a minute. The confidence of the returning veterans was also bolstered because of one addition—their newly anointed point guard, Marion Jones.

Finally, it was time for the season to begin. Not wanting to put too much pressure on her freshman star immediately, Coach Hatchell decided to bring Marion off the bench in the opener. She wound up playing just 21 minutes in her first collegiate game. When it ended, Carolina had a victory with Marion scoring 16 points and garnering 8 assists. The assist total was even more important than the scoring. A point guard is supposed to distribute the ball. That was the area in which Marion lacked experience, yet by dishing out eight assists in a little more than half a game, she more than showed she was ready to assume the role of floor leader.

By the fourth game of the season Marion was the starting point guard and her new teammates had complete confidence in her ability to do the job. Veteran Tonya Sampson spoke for many when she said, "[Marion] understood the game. It was just a matter of changing her attitude from being a shooter to a point guard, realizing she didn't have to score. Once she got that in her head, we were home free."

It was apparent almost from the first that the Lady Tar Heels had one of the best teams in the country. The chant "National Champions" that the players would sound at practices might not be so far-fetched. With the returning players from the 23-7 team a year older and better, the club had a more than solid nucleus. The final piece to the puzzle was Marion, who was making an increasing impact as the season wore on. Not only was she directing the offense with poise and intelligence, but she was already becoming a defensive presence as well.

Because of her great speed, opposing teams often thought twice before making long crosscourt or downcourt passes. They never knew when Marion would come from nowhere and pick the ball off. If she got the ball in the open court with a lane to the basket, no one could catch her. She also became more vocal as the season progressed and always stood up for her teammates, looking for something positive, even when someone made a mistake.

With Marion firmly entrenched at point guard, the Lady Tar Heels raced through the regular season with just two losses, both to the University of Virginia. Next came the Atlantic Coast Conference (ACC) tournament, the winner getting an automatic bid for the postseason NCAA tournament, which would culminate in the national championship game.

Sure enough, the ACC final came down to Carolina facing Virginia once again. Before the game, Coach Hatchell reminded the team that they had never won a conference championship since she had been coaching. All of the players wanted it very badly, but no one more than the talented freshman point guard.

"The intensity in Marion's eyes was like daggers going through my body," Coach Hatchell said. "We hadn't even gone out to warm up yet and she had tears rolling down her face."

Teammate Sylvia Crawley said the other team members fed off Marion's intensity. "When I saw her, I couldn't help crying, too," she said. "It was contagious. We wanted to win so bad it hurt."

On the court, the Lady Tar Heels matched their intensity from the locker room. They ran Virginia off the court, winning easily, 77–60, and then got ready for the big one, the NCAA tournament. They were a step closer to that national title. Then, in the tournament, the team looked very sharp, winning their early games easily. The only close one was a 73–69 win over Vanderbilt, a game in which the team played without Charlotte Smith, who was serving a one-game suspension as the result of a fight in the previous game.

Finally the team was on the brink of the championship. In the title game they would be facing Louisiana Tech, a team that was coming in with a 25-game winning streak. The game was played on April 3, 1994, at the Richmond Coliseum in Virginia, and would turn out to be one of the most dramatic and memorable games in women's basketball history.

The title game took an unexpected turn with less than six minutes gone. That's when Marion was whistled for her third personal foul. After being called for five fouls, a player is out of the game, so Coach Hatchell had no choice but to sit Marion down to save her for later in the game. With their starting point guard out, the Lady Tar Heels got sloppy, turning the ball over and missing easy shots. Fortunately, Louisiana Tech didn't shoot much better and couldn't take advantage of Marion's absence. At the half, the score was tied and the championship still up for grabs.

It was still a low-scoring game, even after Marion returned to start the second half. At one point, Carolina failed to score on 11 straight possessions. With just 5:03 left, Louisiana Tech had taken a 53–48 lead and the Lady Tar Heels began to feel the championship slipping away. Again the pace slowed. Both defenses were tough and good shots few and far between. Carolina clawed its way back to tie the game at 57–all, but Tech's Pam Thomas hit a jump shot to give her team a 59–57 lead with just 15 seconds left. All the pressure was now on North Carolina.

With each tick of the clock bringing the Lady Tar Heels closer to defeat, Marion dribbled upcourt. Then she whipped a pass to Tonya Sampson inside the key and Sampson went up with a short jumper to tie the game. But the ball bounced off the front of the rim. A Louisiana Tech player grabbed it on a bounce, only to have Marion tie her up. The whistle blew for a held ball. There was just 0.7 of a second left. On held balls, possession alternates between the teams. At first, the referee thought the ball belonged to Tech. If that was true, the game was over. But the possession arrow was pointed in the wrong direction and once the error was pointed out, the referee indicated that Carolina had it. With less than a second left, it would take a miracle for the Lady Tar Heels to win.

After a quick time-out to check the Tech defense, which was packed in tight under the hoop, Coach Hatchell decided to go for the win. It would be an all or nothing play. Carolina would try to get the ball to Charlotte Smith for a 3-point try. Stephanie Lawrence would throw the ball in. When she was ready, Tonya Sampson broke to the basket, taking two defenders with her. Smith faked a move toward the hoop, then dropped back beyond the 3-point line. Lawrence whipped the ball to her, and Smith let the shot go just a split second before the buzzer sounded.

It went in!

Smith's buzzer-beater had given Carolina a 60–59 victory and the national championship in perhaps the most incredible finish ever. Marion had been standing at the top of the key during the last-second play, serving as a decoy and drawing another defender away from Smith. She admitted later that she was so nervous she couldn't even move.

"I had never been in a situation where it was all riding on less than a second," she said. "I was glad the play wasn't to me because my hands were frozen on my thighs. . . But it was wonderful. Quite wonderful."

Nothing beats the celebration of a national championship. The players were on cloud nine for weeks, enjoying every moment of their improbable triumph. There was an on-campus parade and then a trip to the White House. Even Carolina's most distinguished basketball alumnus, Michael Jordan, paid a visit to the team and all the players. It was a moment no one who was on the team would ever forget.

As for Marion, she had proved that she was unquestionably ready for big-time college basketball. In 35 games, she averaged 14.1 points, 4.1 rebounds, 3.2 steals, and 2.8 assists a game. Her 494 points and 111 steals were both school records for a freshman. In fact, her steals set a new ACC mark for a first-year player. If there was room for improvement, it would be on the number of assists. But with the team finishing as national champs with a 33-2 record, no one was complaining. As a basketball star, Marion Jones had arrived, and arrived quickly.

Chapter 5
Disappointments

Shortly after she arrived at North Carolina, Marion made an arrangement with track coach Dennis Craddock. She was still intent in pursuing both sports but felt she needed a bit of a break between them. So she told Craddock she would need two weeks off after basketball before she reported for track practice. With the 1993–94 basketball season extending all the way to the national championship game, she missed even more of the track season than she expected.

She still had her great natural talent, but she found that her body wasn't fine-tuned for track. In preparing for basketball, she had bulked up and put on some weight. So while she was still considered a blur on the court, she lost just enough speed to make her vulnerable on the track. Though she won a num-

48

ber of races in dual meets and was named an All-American in her three specialty events (100, 200, and long jump) as well as in the 4 x 100 relay, it was far from the superstar season everyone had envisioned.

For one thing, her best times did not match what she had done as a senior in high school. Her best in the 100 freshman year was 11.28, compared with 11.14 at Thousand Oaks, and 23.00 in the 200, as opposed to 22.58 in high school. While she won the 100 and long jump at the ACC Championships, and finished second in the 200, she had a real disappointment at the NCAA Outdoor Championships. A year earlier, people could have safely predicted that Marion would win three events. Instead, she failed to make the finals of the 100, finished sixth in the 200, and second in the long jump. She was simply not the Marion Jones everyone expected.

Marion admitted that the great success she had in basketball, coupled with the euphoria of winning the national championship, had a negative effect on her track season. "My heart wasn't in it," she explained. "I didn't have enough time to practice and was just going through the motions. Subconsciously, I still expected to compete at a high level and when I couldn't do that, it was tough.

"If anything, I would have thought it would be the other way around. I would have thought track would be great and basketball would be pretty good. It was the exact opposite."

Coach Craddock was also disappointed. He knew

he was getting the best high school sprinter in the nation, a hardworking girl who would get better and better. Though he knew she was committed to playing two sports, he still figured her love of track would put her out there full-time.

"I guess I was hoping that after a year or so she would see she wasn't going to be as good in basketball," he said, "but after that first year I knew it wasn't going to happen. If another great athlete came to me and asked to play two sports, I'd have to think about it long and hard."

So would Marion. In her sophomore year the Lady Tar Heels seemed poised for another great season. Joining the team was another star freshman, Tracy Reid, who would wind up setting a career-scoring record at Carolina before becoming Rookie of the Year with the WNBA's Charlotte Sting. As soon as Reid began practicing with the team, Marion knew she was a great player with whom she could mesh perfectly. It was almost as if the two had a form of ESP. Each seemed to know the other's next move before it was made. Many times Marion would throw a pass just as Tracy began cutting to the basket, and in running the fast break, the two were almost perfection. Their work together made the 1994–95 season even more fun.

The team had a 30-5 record, winning the ACC tournament, but then lost in the sweet sixteen round of the NCAA tourney. Still, it was another fine year. Tracy Reid became the team's leading scorer, but

Marion wasn't far behind. She averaged 17.9 points per game and her 628 total points enabled her to become the only Carolina player to reach the 1,000 point mark in her sophomore season. Her rebounds were up to 5.0 per game and her assist total of 168 was an average of 4.5 per game. Even her steals were up, to 124, and she was named an Honorable Mention All-American by the Associated Press, as well as a First Team All-Atlantic Coast Conference selection.

So it had been yet another successful basketball season. There was little doubt now that Marion had the skills to go from North Carolina straight to the WNBA if she chose. The problem was track. What now? Her body was still geared to basketball and there was no indication that she would be any more successful than she had been the year before. In fact, she seemed to regress even more her sophomore year, losing in the sprints in dual meets and not looking very strong in the long jump.

"Here was this person who used to come down the runway and just power her way into the pit," said Doug Speck, who was the director of the Arcadia Invitational meet. "Watching her now, it looked as if she could barely get off the ground."

At the end of the year there wasn't much left. She managed to win the long jump at the ACC Championships, but her winning jump was just 20'10.5". Then in one of the heats for the 100, she false started twice and was disqualified. She made the 200-meter final, but dropped out before it was run. At the NCAA Championships, the best she could do was a fourth-place finish in the long jump. Suddenly, it began to look as if her track career was going away quickly. It couldn't have come at a worse time. Her original plan was to give up basketball in the 1995–96 season, concentrate on track, compete for North Carolina that spring, then try out for the 1996 Olympic Games.

Many wondered if she would change her mind now, for while her track career seemed to be in decline, her basketball career was definitely still on the upswing. Some thought it was time to give up track and simply parlay her great collegiate basketball career into the pros. There was little doubt that she was good enough. Only Marion still had the dream that was kindled back in 1984. She wanted to compete in the Olympic Games. Before school let out for the summer, Marion told Coach Hatchell that she would stick to her original plan. She would not be playing for the Lady Tar Heels in her junior year.

She returned to California for the summer and moved in with Elliott Mason and his family. Working with Mason again, her zeal for the sport returned quickly. Within weeks, her speed began to return and she felt once again that she had a chance to make her dream come true. She was already thinking in terms of trying to qualify for both the 100 and the 200, and maybe even the long jump. Then, in August, fate once again took a hand.

Marion received a call from Sylvia Hatchell. Her coach told her that the United States basketball team that would be competing at the World University Games needed a point guard. Everyone on the team, as well as the coach, wanted Marion. She told her coach she was now training in earnest for a chance to go to the Olympics. Hatchell said she understood, but also told Marion it was a great chance for her to do something special and to be part of the United States national team. Marion thought about it. She felt she was already back in shape for track, so what harm would playing basketball for a couple of weeks do? She told Coach Hatchell to count her in and promptly flew to Colorado Springs to join the team that was already practicing for the competition.

In one of her first practices Marion dove for a ball that was going out of bounds. One of her teammates dove, as well, and landed on Marion's foot. When she was examined by a doctor she got the bad news. She had fractured the fifth metatarsal bone on the outside of her left foot. There would be no trip to the World University Games. Worse yet, this latest disappointment could possibly put a crimp in her Olympic plans. She was flown back to Chapel Hill where a surgeon inserted a screw in the bone, and put the foot in a cast. The doctor was optimistic. He said the foot would be healed in plenty of time for her to resume her training for the Olympics.

Because the doctors had told her she would heal for the Olympics, Marion fought off any feelings of depression and jumped into the rehabilitation program that had been mapped out for her. She rode a stationary bike, did a great deal of stretching and swimming. The foot felt as if it was healing, and doctors monitored her progress carefully. In December 1995, Marion had another set of X-rays taken and the news couldn't have been better. Doctors said the fracture had healed and gave her the green light to begin some easy workouts.

She began jogging, carefully and slowly at first, and felt she was back on track. She wasn't concerned about her speed returning. After all, look how much progress she had made that summer working with Elliott Mason again. Once more, her Olympic dream seemed closer to reality, and was looking more attainable by the day. Now she also began to think about the long jump. How could she do some light exercise to begin preparing for that additional event? She decided to work out on the trampoline in the gym. It would give her the sense of jumping, but with minimum impact. Or so she thought.

"I had just started the workout," Marion said, "jumping up and down and getting the feel of the trampoline. Then I lost my balance a bit and came down awkwardly. As soon as my foot hit I felt a pop and heard a squeaking sound. When I tried to jump again, I couldn't. . . . I knew I had rebroken the foot."

Sure enough, Marion had fractured the same

bone in the same place. Just that little off-landing on the trampoline had bent the screw that had been inserted in the bone. University surgeon Tim Taft said it was extremely rare for someone to bend a surgical screw, and unheard of in a fracture that had healed. Once again he had to operate on the foot, this time inserting a larger screw. To help the fracture heal faster, he also used some bone marrow that he extracted from Marion's hip. The procedure was successful, but the prognosis was devastating.

Forget the Olympics. That was out. Now Marion would miss the basketball season, but not for the reason she intended. In addition, she would not be able to compete in track and had no chance of making the United States Olympic team. Soon the depression returned. Once again Marion Jones, athlete supreme, couldn't play, couldn't compete, couldn't enjoy the thing she loved the most.

Without their star point guard in the lineup, the North Carolina basketball team struggled all year, finishing the season with a very mediocre, 13-14 record. They weren't even a winning team.

"It hurt not being able to play, not practicing, not scrimmaging, not even sharing their ups and downs," Marion said. "My foot was in a cast and I could hardly walk around."

It was probably the worst time of her life. The second foot fracture seemed to be the last in a series of disappointments that were wearing her down. Unable to play sports and with her Olympic dream shattered, Marion even lost interest in school. Her grades dropped and suddenly her future, which had always looked so bright, was filled with question marks. It was time for something good to happen and when it did, it was a complete surprise to everyone, even Marion.

Chapter 6
C.J.

Despite her depression, Marion began to slowly do the only thing she could. She began to rehab the foot while trying to keep in the best shape possible under the circumstances. Part of her routine was to work out in the weight room. Even with the broken foot, there were many upper body exercises she could do.

Despite her depression, Marion began to slowly do the only thing she could. She began to rehab the foot while trying to keep in the best shape possible under the circumstances. Part of her routine was to work out in the weight room. Even with the broken foot, there were many upper body exercises she could do. It was in the North Carolina weight room that winter where she met C. J. Hunter for the first time. Hunter was a world-class shot-putter who had won a bronze medal at the 1995 World Championships. He, too, had Olympic ambitions. That winter, he was an assistant track coach at Carolina working with the shot-putters and discus and javelin throwers. That meant working them out in the weight room.

At first, Marion and C.J just said a casual *Hi!* to each other. C.J. had also watched the women's basketball team play quite often that year, and he heard the stories about how much better they would have been if Marion Jones were in the lineup. He also knew, of course, about Marion's reputation in track. When Marion began going to track practice early in 1996, she was still very limited in what she could do. Much of her time was spent watching and pretty soon she began talking with C.J. on a regular basis. She found him incredibly knowledgeable about the entire sport and soon enjoyed talking with him about the analytical aspects of track and field.

One day C.J. gave her a ride to the airport and she also learned that he could make her laugh. Suddenly, this big, three hundred-pound man was making it easier for her to deal with her depression and injury. Soon they began seeing more of each other, going to dinner, to movies, and spending a great deal of time just talking. There was, however, one problem. University rules did not allow coaches to date students. While the two kept a low profile at first, it wasn't long before the word got out. Marion was seeing C.J. and he was a coach.

Finally, Coach Craddock called C.J. into his office and said he was forced to give him an ultimatum. Because of the university rules, he would have to stop dating Marion or resign his position as an assistant coach. It took the big man just an instant to decide. He told Coach Craddock he would resign.

"It was an easy call," he said, later. "It was not a big deal."

Marion was upset at first, wondering why he would walk away from something he obviously loved. He told her there would be other coaching opportunities, but he wasn't about to be told he couldn't see her. The relationship would continue, though it wouldn't be easy. For one thing, C.J. was nearly seven years older than she was. He also had an ex-wife and two young children living in Colorado. In addition, C.J. was an intimidating man, not too talkative, and very blunt. There were people worried about the relationship from the beginning.

Even Marion admitted she thought about these things at first. "I thought about how seeing C.J. would affect me," she said. "But I thought back then that this was just a guy I was dating and we were having fun together."

Because she was seeing C.J., Marion made it a point to go to the 1996 Olympics in Atlanta. After all, he was on the team, competing in the shot put. Besides watching C.J., she also found herself watching the sprinters and once again admiring runners like Gail Devers and Gwen Torrence. She thought about trying out for the team in 1992 when she was still in high school and the disappointment of not even getting the chance this time because of her injury. She was already planning to return to the Carolina basketball team in the fall, but she also missed track. After all, it had been her first love.

Once again there would be the decision of picking one sport over another, or continuing with both. C.J.

was smart enough not to pressure Marion. He felt she might decide to return to track, but knew it would have to be a decision only she could make. She would just need some more time.

Coming back to the Lady Tar Heels wasn't difficult. Her skills returned quickly and she fit in like a glove. Once again Coach Hatchell had a very good team. With Marion back, it was close to being a great team. They wound up with a 29-3 record and were nationally ranked. Once again they won the ACC tournament, with Marion named the tourney's MVP. They were then the number one seed in the east regionals of the NCAA tournament. It was felt they had a good chance to win another national championship.

However, in tournament game against Michigan State, one of the Carolina stars, Jessica Gaspar, suffered a knee injury that ended her season. The Lady Tar Heels won the game in overtime, but when they played George Washington University in the next round, they were upset, 46–44, in a rather sloppy game. Marion finished with just eight points and no assists, saying that the GW defense had shut her down.

It had still been a fine year. After missing the previous season, she bounced back to average a career high 18.6 points. Her other numbers were down somewhat from two years earlier, but she was still named a First Team All-American by *Basketball America* and was a Third Team selection by the Associated Press. Then, immediately after the final game, Marion let her teammates know her intentions.

Though it was her fourth year at North Carolina and she was slated to graduate in a few months, the injury the year before gave her another season of eligibility. All she would have to do was enroll in graduate school and she could play again. Coach Hatchell had already spoken to her about the outstanding recruiting class that would be coming in and felt the Lady Tar Heels could once again challenge for the national title . . . especially if Marion returned.

But in the locker room after the loss to George Washington, Marion spoke to the team. She told the other players that she loved being at North Carolina and her days on the basketball team would always be special. Her teammates, she said, were like sisters to her and always would be. But now she had decided to return to track full-time and to pursue her dream of running in the Olympics. There were tears and hugs all over, a lot of sad goodbyes, but Marion had made her decision and it was final.

Marion also decided not to compete in track for Carolina that spring and her decision left a lot of hard feelings on several fronts. Many seemed to feel that her decision was strongly influenced by C.J. Hunter and had she not met him, she would have continued to compete for the school. Those people, however, didn't really know Marion. Sure, she listened to the input of others, but in the end she was her own person and always made her own decisions.

The problems had started the year she was hurt. She wasn't getting along with her mother, feeling she wanted to be on her own, "wanted to be free." Yet her mother lived just 10 minutes from her dorm, not always a good situation. Her relationship with track coach Craddock deteriorated because he didn't visit her when she broke her foot. By that time she had moved to an off-campus apartment and when her grades began to fall when she was depressed about the injury, Coach Hatchell tried to order her to move back to the dorm. The coach also disapproved of her relationship with C.J. So Marion felt the circle was beginning to close.

Then, when she told Coach Hatchell early in 1997 that she was thinking about leaving school and not returning to play another year, there were conflicting stories of how each reacted. According to some, the coach told Marion she understood and that she could make more money in professional track than in the new women's professional basketball leagues that were just getting started then. She said she didn't try to talk Marion out of leaving.

Marion, on the other hand, said the coach didn't take the news well and tried to talk her into changing her mind, reminding her that she hadn't had great success in track in years, while she was a sure-shot to make it in the WNBA. She, too, Marion said, thought C. J. Hunter was pressuring her to leave.

Hunter, for his part, was very candid in his observations. "People who criticize us don't [care] about Marion," he said. "[Coach] Hatchell was just thinking of her own team."

Ironically, the 1997–98 Lady Tar Heels made it to the final eight in the NCAA tournament. There they met defending champion Tennessee and were up by 12 points with some seven minutes remaining. But the Lady Vols rallied and finally won the game by a 76–70 count. Marion's old friend Tracy Reid, who was now an All-American and ACC Player of the Year, played her heart out in that game. When it became apparent near the end that Carolina was going to lose, Reid had one thought running through her mind. "I was thinking," she said, "if only Marion was here. If we only had Marion."

But basketball was over, at least for a while. Now it was time to attack her track career in a serious way. The only setback occurred at the end of April. At the time, C.J. had a deal with Nike that gave him equipment and a small amount of money for training, as well as performance bonuses. Otherwise, he and Marion's only other income came from what he could win on the tour. Occasionally, he would get some help from his agent, Charlie Wells. So they were living pretty close to the vest.

Nike was also becoming interested in Marion. Knowing her past record and her achievements as a teenager, the Beaverton, Oregon, company felt she had the potential to excel once again and was watching her closely. Then, in April, a Nike representative invited her to run on a relay team at the prestigious Penn Relays. Just before the meet, she was told that Dennis Craddock, the track coach at North Carolina, had called to say that she was still eligible to compete for the school and, since she was still on scholarship, she could not wear the colors of a sporting goods company while still at school. Just to play it safe, she was advised not to run.

The entire incident angered her. As it turned out, Craddock was wrong. For one thing, Marion's scholarship was for basketball, and that season was over. In addition, the NCAA rules were geared to accommodate seniors who were no longer competing and close to graduating. There was little chance North Carolina would dismiss her with graduation imminent and just a few months remaining on her scholarship. The fact that Craddock had even tried to stop her from running left a sour taste in her mouth about her entire track career at North Carolina. After that, she didn't even train at the school anymore. At that point, she was closer to C. J. Hunter than ever.

"When you try to keep two people apart, what happens?" Hunter asked, rhetorically. "They become closer."

That's what happened. Marion graduated from North Carolina with a degree in journalism and communications. She had become an All-American basketball player and had the joy of helping her team win a national championship. Track had been a disappointment, but now she was ready to change all that. She was also ready to burst on to the national track scene in a very dramatic way.

Chapter 7
Becoming Number One

As soon as Marion went into rigorous training in April 1997, she realized there was a great deal of work to be done. Being in great shape for basketball is not the same as being in great shape for sprinting and long jumping. As she said, she could run up and down the basketball court all day without getting tired, but as soon as she began track workouts, she noticed the difference.

"Just running around the track made me use muscles I hadn't used in four years," she said.

She also began an intense weight-training program under C.J.'s guidance. She had to get stronger, but also had to lose weight. For basketball, Marion usually weighed about 165 pounds. The weight didn't affect her court speed and allowed her to better absorb the pounding that goes along with the court game. A finely tuned sprinter, however, simply cannot carry any extra weight. To be at her best on the track, Marion usually weighed between 145 and 150 pounds, so she was still some 20 pounds overweight.

Because of her not-so-amicable parting of the ways with her coaches at North Carolina, Marion and C.J. shifted their workouts to Paul Derr Field, which was located at North Carolina State University. When she decided to go to NC State, Marion didn't realize that there were already a group of top track performers there, as well as a coach who would help change her life.

His name was Trevor Graham, a native of Jamaica whose family had come to the United States when he was fourteen. Graham became a fine quartermiler who won the NCAA Division II Championship in that event in 1987. At the 1988 Olympics in Seoul, Graham was part of the Jamaican 4 x 400 relay team that won the silver medal, finishing behind a record-setting United States team. He subsequently became an assistant track coach at Kansas State University. Then he set out to learn all he could about the techniques of running, starting with how the body utilizes oxygen—everything that could make a runner improve performance. Gradually, he formulated his own ideas and theories.

By 1991, Graham was working in Raleigh as a security officer while looking for athletes to coach. His wife, Ann, was a ranked 400-meter hurdler who wanted to make the 1992 United States Olympic team. But with a teaching job and a young child at home, she just didn't have the time to make a full commitment. She got as far as a semifinal before being eliminated. Though disappointed, her husband continued to seek out other athletes. By the time he came to Paul Derr Field, he was working with some dozen or so top runners, including world-class 400-meter star Antonio Pettigrew. His reputation was growing.

Trevor Graham was already somewhat familiar with Marion. He had seen her run while she was at Thousand Oaks, and had watched some of her basketball games on television. He had also met C.J. previously. One day the two men began talking as Marion was working out. C.J. saw that Graham couldn't stop watching her and was impressed.

"I could see how powerful she was," Graham said. "She was so much more explosive than any woman I've seen since Florence Griffith-Joyner. She was still a little overweight from basketball and her technique needed work, but her talent and competitiveness was something that can't be taught."

C.J. then asked Graham if he had any suggestions. He quickly replied that he did, describing to C.J. what he would do. C.J. suggested he show Marion. Graham quickly gave her a few tips about coming out of the blocks when she started and she sensed immediately that he was right. It was apparent to everyone that they were on the same wavelength, clicking immediately, but it took C.J. to say the words.

"Why don't you coach her?" he suggested.

It was, as they say, the beginning of a beautiful friendship. Marion turned out to be the perfect student, and Graham the wise teacher. He began to work with her on every phase of the race, teaching her to be more relaxed, yet to use her natural size, strength, and explosiveness. Before the 1997 season even began, her time in the 100 was down to 11.19, very close to what she had run in high school. Graham felt that she was almost ready to drop it below 11, which would put her right up with the world's elite sprinters.

Graham also felt that the years of basketball had helped her become more explosive and aggressive. Now she had to retool her thinking to track. In basketball, he reasoned, you are working so that the team can win. In track, you are working so that you can win. It's a slightly different mindset, but Marion was getting there. Because she had been away from track for so long, with basketball and her injury, she had fresh legs and a renewed love of the sport. Some youngsters, who concentrate only on track during their formative years, can find themselves burning out by the time they reach their early twenties, the prime years.

After a couple of mediocre times in her first meets, Marion began to make major strides. Running at the Tennessee Invitational at Knoxville on May 24, she won the 100 in 10.98 seconds, a personal best.

"We were all going crazy," Marion said. "Trevor, C.J., and I. Finishing under 11 seconds for the first time told us that bigger things were going to happen. I knew I was ready to do something special."

Within a short time, Marion signed a deal with Nike, a sure sign that her star was rising and a move that would help her financially. Now she could concentrate on her running. Trevor Graham was another who felt great things were just ahead. When a reporter called him after the Tennessee Invitational and asked how fast he thought Marion might run the 100 before the season ended, Graham answered quickly, saying he felt she would run a 10.76.

It was a shocking prediction. The world record in the 100 had been that same 10.76, until Florence Griffith-Joyner ran her amazing 10.49 at the 1988 Olympics. Only Joyner, Merlene Ottey, and Evelyn Ashford had ever run that fast. Graham was predicting, in effect, that Marion would be entering a select circle . . . and very soon. The story broke just before the United States National Championships in Indianapolis that June. That put some added pressure on Marion, as well as opening her up to the same question from almost every reporter there. She tried to joke about it.

"I told [Trevor] that if he's ever going to make predictions again to let me know first," she told the press.

Now Marion had to perform. When she lined up for the first heat in the 100, the crowd grew quiet. It was as if every eye was on her, waiting to see if she would challenge one of the best times ever run. Marion burst out of the blocks and powered her way down the track. She crossed the finish line first in a time of 10.98. It wasn't 10.76, but it wasn't that far away. There were still two more races to go.

In the semifinals, Marion did even better. This time she crossed the finish line in 10.92. Those watching could tell she was still accelerating at the finish. She was beginning to feel she could win in the final, too. There was one minor disappointment when Marion learned that Gail Devers had withdrawn from the final with a calf injury. She wanted to run against the best. But Devers or not, there was still a race to run and she felt she was ready.

Once again she burst out of the blocks and began chewing up the track with her long strides. Despite running into a head wind, she felt her power and her confidence grow. When she hit the tape she knew she had won. Her time was 10.97. It had been just three months since Marion had rededicated herself to her track career and now she was a national champion. Even her competition couldn't believe she had come so far so fast.

"We all knew she was fast," said third-place finisher Inger Miller. "But we also knew it takes years to reach a high level. Everyone was shocked how quickly she hit those times."

Next she had to compete in the long jump against the legendary Jackie Joyner-Kersee. Marion had admired Jackie for so long that she felt a bit nervous competing against her. Then on her first jump, she soared 22' 3¾", some two inches farther than her previous best. Despite continued poor technique and awkward landings, she took the early lead. With each competitor getting six jumps, it was far from over. Her lead held up, however, until Joyner-Kersee's fifth jump. The veteran hit a good one, going 22' 8" and taking over the lead.

Then, on Marion's last jump, she really went for it, not worrying about fouling or technique. She sped down the runway, hit the board, and leaped as far as she could. When the judges took the measurement, they found they had a winner. Marion had jumped 22' 9" to win the competition by one inch. It was her second win in the Nationals and the first person to congratulate her was Jackie Joyner-Kersee.

"There are so many of us who do great things on the athletic field and we just forget other people exist," Joyner-Kersee told a reporter, afterward. "And that's sad. Even though she belongs on the pedestal, [Marion] doesn't act like she owns the pedestal."

Marion was on the map. Charlie Wells, C.J.'s agent, was representing Marion as well, and he soon began getting offers for her to run in Europe. She decided to compete in several meets overseas, leading up to the World Championships. To do that, she had to learn to deal with new things. The travel wasn't easy. Sometimes the athletes were overcome by jet lag. The accommodations weren't always great, and in some places not many people spoke English. European athletes were ferocious competitors. Track was the way they made their living. The better they did, the more money they made. Marion won her early meets, though her times weren't that great.

In Lausanne, Switzerland, she finally had a chance to run head-to-head against Gail Devers. Devers had won the 100 in both the 1992 and 1996 Olympics, and was still one of the world's best. Would the young upstart be able to beat the wily veteran? It was a great race, Marion coming in with a new personal best of 10.90. But in her excitement she let her technique fall apart and Devers won in a close finish. Coach Graham was quick to point out the mistakes she made, telling her that had she maintained her technique, she would have won.

Two days later, in a much slower race in Oslo, Marion did beat Devers. It didn't matter that her time was 11.06. She had conquered yet another barrier, beating the two-time Olympic champion. Now everything was pointing to Athens, Greece, and the World Championships.

During this time, Marion and C.J. had become even closer. He wasn't just with her to watch, he was busy competing in the shot put. Away from the track the two were nearly inseparable and pretty much kept to themselves. "You almost never see Marion outside of her room on the circuit," said Inger Miller, "and if you do, she's with C.J."

Marion couldn't have been happier. "I've never in my life had somebody whom I could tell everything to," she said. "Now I can. I have a companion."

There were still some who felt Marion's life was now being directed by C.J. Jackie Joyner-Kersee had heard similar statements when she married Bobby Kersee, who doubled as her coach and often drove her hard to excel. "There are plenty of people who have never liked me and Bobby together," Jackie said. "It doesn't matter. Marion and C.J. are a partnership. It's their life, and outsiders don't matter."

That's how Marion and C.J. were playing it. It was their life and they were determined to do it their way. So far, everything was working. Now it was on to Athens and the Worlds.

It was very hot, a crowded and noisy atmosphere that could be intimidating to an inexperienced runner. The early heats in the 100 were held in the morning and evening. Marion ran an 11.03 in the morning, and a 10.96 in the evening, winning both heats.

The next day came the semifinals. Competing in Marion's heat was thirty-seven-year-old Merlene Ottey, the veteran from Jamaica who was still one of the world's best. Marion seemed to catch the electricity of the moment and blazed home in 10.94 seconds to win the heat. Ottey was second in 11.08. Some felt Marion had run too fast. The purpose of the heat is to make sure you qualify for the next round. Many runners ease up a bit when they know they've got a qualifying spot clinched. Marion had gone all out.

In the final, there was a false start. Ottey didn't hear the second report of the starter's gun, which signaled the false start, and ran half the distance at full speed before she realized what had happened. That took too much out of her. When they started again, Marion came out of the blocks well and quickly reached her full stride. She was pulling ahead. Thinking she had it won, she began to ease up slightly about twenty-five meters from the finish. Suddenly, she sensed someone coming up fast. She tried to kick it up a notch, lost of bit of her technique, and leaned to the tape at the end. It had been Zhanna Pintusevich of the Ukraine who had made a gallant effort to catch Marion. The judges reviewed the finish quickly and declared Marion the winner. Her time was a personal best of 10.83, very close to Trevor Graham's prediction of 10.76. Had she not eased up a bit, she might have even run faster than the predicted mark.

Though she didn't do well in the long jump, finishing in tenth place, she returned to run the second leg of the victorious 4 x 100 relay team. She joined Chryste Gaines, Inger Miller, and Gail Devers in winning another gold medal. So Marion Jones had come, had seen, and had conquered. Less than a half year after returning to track, she was now being called the fastest woman in the world. Then, several weeks later, competing in a meet in Brussels, Belgium, Marion blazed down the track in the 100, crossing the finish in 10.76 seconds! She had made Trevor Graham's prediction come true. In the long history of women's track and field, only Florence Griffith-Joyner had run a faster 100 meters. Would that record be next?

Chapter 8

The Amazing Marion Jones

Things couldn't have gone better for Marion in 1997. Not only had she reestablished herself as a world-class track star, but she had come all the way to the head of the class. Though she had concentrated on the 100 most of the time, she also ran a personal best of 21.76 in the 200. Only the long jump wasn't quite where she wanted it to be. That was the event that would prove the most difficult for Marion, even in the years ahead.

While 1998 was the one year out of four without either the Olympic Games or World Championships, Marion and C.J. decided to stay very busy. Marion was getting offers from all over the world and her appearance fees were rising rapidly. C.J. was still a topflight shot-putter who continued to work to improve his distance. Contrary to what some had thought, he did not stop his own career to manage Marion's.

When they finally drew up their schedule, it was an incredibly busy one. She would be traveling to Australia and Japan, competing in North Carolina and California, then traveling back to Japan, to China, and then home to Oregon. In June it would be Finland, Italy, back to New Orleans. Then Austria, Norway, Italy, New York, and France. Keep naming countries and it seemed Marion would be there. Sweden, Monaco, Switzerland, Belgium. Germany, Russia, South Africa. That was through September. After that, Marion and C.J. were planning an October 3 wedding. It was an unbelievable schedule, but Marion thought she could do it. She felt at twenty-two she was close to her peak. She also knew that the next three years would have some huge meets, as well as increasing demands on her time. This was the only year she and C.J. could plan a schedule like this. Why not give it a try?

Her coach, Trevor Graham, also felt the killer schedule was the way to go. "Many people in track and field don't want to compete too much," he said. "They don't want to run against this person or that person. But the way Marion was prepared, we wanted her to take on anyone in the world. And we wanted to do it now. I really thought she could dominate the world."

Talk about great expectations. So off they went and, just as expected, Marion was winning everywhere. Winning with great times and jumps, and winning big. Wherever she went, she was greeted with cheers and admiration. She had become a worldwide celebrity. In each race, she gave her all. Like any performer on a stage, she wanted people seeing her for the first (and maybe only) time to always remember Marion Jones. So she never coasted, never let up, and she never lost. When she arrived in New Orleans that June for the US Nationals, she had not lost a race or a long jump all year. As Trevor Graham had said, she was dominating the world.

In the 100, she put on another great show. Her times were blazing fast and consistent. She won the first heat in 10.75, the semifinals in 10.71—tying her personal best—then won the final in 10.72. Another gold. Even her competitors were feeling a bit overwhelmed.

"There's a big gap between Marion and the rest of us right now," said second-place finisher Chryste Gaines, who ran her own personal best of 10.89. "And I don't think she is going to be coming back any time soon."

The night after winning the 100, Marion felt her legs beginning to cramp a bit. After a good massage and some sound sleep she was ready to go again the next day. All she did on this day was win the 200 with a time of 22.24 into a head wind, then win the long jump with a leap of 23' 8". It was the first time in fifty years that a woman had won three national titles. Marion Jones could be ignored no longer.

For Marion, it had been a grueling competition, but well worth it. "I was exhausted," she said, after competing all weekend in mid-to high-90 degree temperatures. "I'm happy and relieved to come out in this heat and win all three events. I didn't feel any pressure. But it's definitely the most difficult thing I've done. The 100 and long jump took a lot out of me."

Now everything was falling into place. Marion and C.J. had built a new, four-bedroom house in the upscale neighborhood of Apex, midway between Raleigh and Chapel Hill. Of course, they were on the road much of the time, but it was still nice to come home. Not that they were big party types. As C.J. said, a typical day at home was "training, a nap, and 'Judge Judy.'"

Their few good friends included C.J.'s coach, Brian Blutreich, and his wife, as well as some of Marion's former basketball teammates from her North Carolina days. Otherwise, they usually stayed home. All that world traveling could be very wearing, so quiet moments were considered precious and to be savored. The way Marion was performing in 1998, there wouldn't be too much of that quiet time. The crescendo over her performances was building. Everyone wanted Marion Jones.

"She has both athletic ability and charisma," said one sports agent. "That's rare in track and field. It's what sets her apart."

Even her former basketball coach, Sylvia Hatchell,

could see that special quality in Marion. "She's like a movie star," the coach said. "Whatever mood she's in, she can turn it on for the cameras."

Watching her perform at the Nationals, Jackie Joyner-Kersee was full of admiration for Marion's talent. "I don't know what she can't do," said Joyner-Kersee. "She's gifted and she's mentally tough. She can own everything from the 400 on down, plus the long jump."

Perhaps it was her great success and stable life with C.J. that led Marion to mend fences with her mother. The two simply had seen very little of each other during the previous year or so, but when Marion Tolar had eye surgery in April, her daughter visited her every day. Then in May she spent one of her off weeks at her mother's home, which was now in Houston.

"My mother and I love each other very much," Marion said, ending their much-publicized rift. "I'd do anything for her and vice versa. If at the end of my life I can say that I was just a quarter of the woman she has been, I will be satisfied."

There were those who felt Marion had had a great deal of anger over the years. She had never fully come to terms with the fact that her real father had left and never tried to have a relationship with her. The situation at North Carolina that last year, when her coaches seemed to turn on her somewhat, also fueled some bitterness. But now, with her life fully on track, that anger and bitterness seemed to be melting away. She was now beginning to enjoy everything—her relationship with C.J., her tremendous success on the track, and her old friends.

On one of her visits to her mother that year, Marion suddenly gave her a large check. Her mother just shook her head, saying she didn't want her daughter's money, just a good relationship with her. An emotional Marion gestured to her mother that she understood. "Mom," she said. "I want you to have it."

What Marion had achieved in the first months of the 1998 track season firmly established her as one of the sport's top stars. Now, as she resumed competition after the Nationals, talk turned to how fast she could run. Specifically, could she break the great records in the 100 and 200 set by Florence Griffith-Joyner. Marion made no secret of her ultimate goals.

"The majority of women in sprinting have acted like those records can never be broken," she said. "So they haven't pressed to go fast. I'm 22 years old; I'm going to get faster. Before my career is over, I will attempt to run faster than any woman has ever run and jump farther than any woman has ever jumped."

Any great athlete worth his or her salt wants to be the best, to set new limits, to do better than those who have come before. Even some of her competitors were looking to her not only to do great things on the track, but to bring the sport more widespread recognition than it had had in years. Gail Devers, a two-time Olympic champion, was one who felt the charisma of her sport's newest star.

"You can see the excitement when people know Marion is going to compete," Devers said. "I think she's one of the people who's going to bring our sport back to the forefront. She's doing what Florence did ten years ago, setting a new standard. I honestly feel what Marion has brought to track and field for women, and what she will bring, is going to be great for years to come."

In August, a sprinter named Christine Arron won the 100-meter dash at the European Championships in Budapest. More importantly, her time was 10.73, putting her in a class with Marion. The two were slated to meet in Belgium and there was a great deal of hype. Maybe now people would see if Marion Jones was really invincible. Arron, for her part, hyped the race with some good, old-fashioned trash talk. At one point, Arron said that Marion acted as if she was unbeatable, adding, "The first time she loses, it will really shake her confidence."

Arron had been born in Guadeloupe and was now running for France. Apparently, she didn't know about Marion's hard times, the races she had lost while at North Carolina. Reporters, however, kept asking Marion about Arron, time and again, until she finally said, "Let's just race."

The race in Brussels was run into a head wind, cutting down the times. Despite that, it was a one-sided affair. Marion led from the start, used her great stride to open a very solid lead and broke the tape in 10.80 seconds. Arron was several strides behind, finishing in 10.95 seconds, a very large margin in a short race. Once again, Marion had settled the issue where it should be settled. On the track.

The final meet of the year was the World Cup, held in Johannesburg, South Africa, from September 11–13. Marion would have liked nothing better than to end the season by approaching or topping one or both of Flo-Jo's records. She felt she had a chance, because of the conditions under which she would be running.

"I have heard that the track at the Johannesburg stadium is one of the fastest in the world and is at high altitude," she said, in a statement. "That gives me much hope that, [with] my present form, I might challenge for the world 100-meter record."

This time Marion would be running the 200 first. She blazed around the curve and came home in 21.62 seconds, a personal best and the third fastest 200 ever run. She was getting close. The next day she was poised for the 100. Once again she burst out of the blocks and powered down the track. She broke the tape in 10.65 seconds, another personal best and the fourth fastest 100 of all time. Though the high altitude might have helped, she was getting closer to Flo-Jo's standards of 10.49 and 21.34.

Now it was time for the final event, the long jump. It was a cool, rainy afternoon, but Marion was confident. Once again, however, she had problems with her technique and lost to Heike Drechsler of Germany, a veteran and one of the finest long jumpers in track history. Drechsler leaped 23' 2½", while Marion was second—some three inches behind. Amazingly, it was her only loss of the entire season. Equally amazing was the fact that, despite all her victories, it bothered her.

"At the start of training in '98, I made it a point that I wanted to win my last competition," Marion said. "I wanted to be able to rise above it when my body and my mind were tired, and I felt shot. All I could think about was that long jump and how lousy I competed and how it wasn't me. I can't let it happen to me ever again. Or not very often."

Just that statement alone showed the kind of competitor Marion Jones had become. She had spent the entire 1998 season beating all comers despite a tiring, hectic, world-traveling schedule. No one had been able to defeat her in the 100, 200, or long jump . . . until that final event in South Africa. With all the victories, all the challenges met, all the great times, that one loss stuck in her craw. It was that kind of attitude that made everyone think Marion was going to continue to improve, continue to make track history.

How much better could she be than the miracle season of 1998?

Chapter 9
Back to Earth

In some ways, it must seem that whenever too many good things happen, the bad can't be far behind. Despite the loss to Heike Drechsler in the long jump, Marion couldn't have asked for much more. Both her professional and personal lives were on a high, and the arrow still appeared to be pointing up. She was already thinking about the World Championships in 1999 and then the Olympic Games the following year. There weren't a whole lot of negative thoughts.

After the World Cup, she and C.J. returned to the United States for some well-deserved rest. They were back about a week when on the morning of September 21, they received a call from Trevor Graham. The news he had was devastating. He had just heard that Florence Griffith-Joyner had died at the age of thirty-eight. Marion and C.J. couldn't believe it. Unfortunately, it was true. Still a charismatic public figure, a stylish woman who had a clothing line, did charitable work and starred in commercials, Flo-Jo's death shocked everyone. Apparently, she had suffered a seizure in her sleep, vomited, and had suffocated.

"It hurt so much," Marion said. "It hurt because my generation, those of us who are competing now, were so inspired by her. The first time we saw Florence, we were at the stage in our lives where we were very impressionable. To see her compete, to see her break records, and to see her enjoy it so much—to be so confident, so strong—it hurt. I never met her, but I knew her. We all knew her."

There had always been rumors about Flo-Jo. Because she had just one truly marvelous season, the Olympic year in which she set her records, many suspected she had been using performance-enhancing drugs. Despite the fact that she never failed a single drug test, the suspicions were always there. Even in death, reporters awaited the result of the autopsy. Once again, there was no evidence of any kind of drug in her body. Her death was just a tragic accident.

Flo-Jo's death put a damper on the entire track world, as well as with others who knew and were touched by her. Marion and C.J., though feeling the loss deeply, went ahead with their plans and were married on October 3. The relationship that so many felt wouldn't work had come full circle.

Several months later, Marion met Al Joyner, Flo-Jo's husband and Jackie Joyner-Kersee's brother, at a dinner in New York where Marion received the Jesse Owens Award as the outstanding woman track athlete in the United States. He told Marion that he and Flo-Jo had always followed Marion's career. They admired her because of the way she put her track career on hold to play basketball, the way she came back from injuries, and the way she set her goals of breaking Flo-Jo's records. In other words, Marion followed her own star and that impressed them.

Hearing that from Al Joyner made Marion feel good, and while it didn't temper her sense of loss at Flo-Jo's untimely death, it gave her an even better feeling about the woman whose records she knew she would continue to chase.

In fact, by this time she had already mapped out her goals for the next two years. For one thing, she said she planned to remain in the sport "as long as it takes to go after Florence's records."

But that wasn't all. She said her 1999 plans included going after four gold medals at the World Championships, slated to be held in Seville, Spain, in August. She predicted she would compete in the 100, 200, long jump, and 4 x 1600 relay, and hoped for golds in each. Her goals for the 2000 Olympics were even more ambitious. Marion said flat out she would try to do something never before achieved by an Olympic track athlete. She would try to win five, yes five gold medals—in the 100, 200, long jump, 4 x 100 relay, and 4 x 400 relay. It was a statement that immediately turned heads.

"Five golds is not just talk," she told the press. "It's possible. If any athlete can do it, it's myself. I was born with a lot of talent, but I'm also a very hard worker. I love to win, I loved to be on top, I love the feeling of crossing the finish line first, about five or six meters ahead of everyone else. It's good to be considered one of the greatest ever. It's not going to happen overnight. It will take a lot of hard work."

So the die was cast. Many athletes, even if they had set these kinds of lofty goals, would hesitate to make them public. After all, if they didn't reach them they would open themselves up to criticism. Marion, like many great ones, wasn't afraid to fail. She had the confidence and belief in herself, and honestly thought she could do it. If not, there would be no excuses.

She was already a prohibitive favorite in the 100 and 200. With the abundance of fine sprinters and runners in the United States, it was a good bet that both relay teams would be tracking gold. The biggest problem she might have would undoubtedly be the long jump. She still was having problems with her technique and needed a great deal of work. Her progress in the long jump hadn't matched her running. Many knowledgeable track people, however, wouldn't bet against her.

Al Joyner, himself a former Olympic triple-jump champion, felt that Marion had the potential to be a record-setting long jumper. "I think she will jump at least 25 feet," Joyner said. "Once she maximizes her speed and her power, she'll be unbelievable. Once she masters her speed on the board, she'll go into orbit."

So the stage was almost set. Marion planned to begin her 1999 season slowly. It wouldn't be like 1998. She would schedule only a handful of meets before June and cut back on the number of events she would enter. The focal point of her season would be the World Championships. That meet, she felt, would be a barometer to gauge her chances to win five golds at the Olympics.

Besides the long jump, some wondered if she would qualify for the 4 x 400 relay. Marion had some good times in the 400-meter run, but never concentrated on the event. In fact, she always said she hated it. "It hurts too much," she said. "I have no control of my body afterwards. I can't breathe, I can't sit, I can't walk. I like running [the distance] in the relay. It's a completely different feeling when you're trying to chase somebody down."

Yet in April, she entered the Mount San Antonio College Relays near Los Angeles and entered the 400-meter run. The field wasn't very strong, with Marion the favorite. Running the event she hated, she blew the opposition away and crossed the line in 50.79 seconds, the second fastest time in the world at that point in 1999. The time was more than good enough to qualify her for a spot on the 4 x 400 relay team at the World Championships. She was right on course for 2000.

Marion continued to compete at a few select meets during the early part of the year. She joined some of her fellow competitors in trying to drum up more support for a sport that had been in decline with the public in the United States for a number of years. There was a time when a major track and field meet would receive solid support, both from the fans in attendance and on television. But for some reason, the fan base was eroding, despite performers like Marion Jones, Michael Johnson, Maurice Greene, Gail Devers, Jackie Joyner-Kersee, and other American stars. European, Asian, and African track-and-field performers were idolized as national heroes. Then again, those countries didn't have baseball, football, and basketball as major sports. Maybe there were just too many sports in the United States. There were the aforementioned big three, then hockey, golf, and tennis. Track and field had become a weak sister. Even the Atlanta Olympics in 1996 didn't start a trend.

When Marion was set to compete in the Penn Relays at the end of April, she voiced her disappointment with the public support for her sport. "It's not too often as American athletes that we can stay home and go to a track meet," she said. "We love to compete in front of all the people and the Penn Relays is definitely a highlight for me. I know growing up, watching the Penn Relays on television was a highlight, to see the young kids competing."

But that year there was no television. Not one single part of the three-day event would appear on the tube. Another example was the first TFA Pro Championships, held in Uniondale, New York in June. The meet drew a sparse crowd of just 3,184 fans. Marion won the 100 and said it was nice to get a victory, but "a little disappointing that not more people were here. But it will take some time to get spectators out to an event such as this."

Some already saw Marion as a possible savior, bringing the same attention to track and field that Tiger Woods had brought to golf. She had the talent and charisma, same as Woods, and if she could stay on course for all those gold medals, she should begin to bring out legions of new fans. The sport certainly needed someone like her, especially in the United States. Then if there were a few more runners to challenge her, to set up a continuing rivalry, it could only help the sport.

On June 10, Marion competed in her first European meet of the summer, flying to Helsinki, Finland, where she won the 200. The original plan was to make that the last meet before the US Track and Field Championships, slated for Eugene, Oregon, two weeks later. But on June 12, the day after arriving home, she decided to enter the long jump in the Pontiac Grand Prix Invitational at Raleigh. It was far from a major meet, with few big stars, but Marion wanted to compete because it was held alongside the two-day national high school track-and-field championships. She felt her support for high school track was important.

Once again, Marion was having trouble with her long jump technique. With just one jump remaining, she was behind Adrien Sawyer. The Texas A&M jumper was ranked just eleventh in the United States. Naturally, the competitive fires in Marion were burning and she didn't want to lose. Before her last jump, Coach Graham told her to start half a foot back, then just give it all she had. Don't worry about technique until you're in the air, he told her.

Marion blasted it, all right, soaring twenty-three feet even to win by nearly eight inches. There was only one problem. She landed awkwardly and hurt her right knee. C.J. rushed over and carried her out of the pit, but Marion insisted he put her down so people could see her walk off the field, which she did. Fortunately, it wasn't a serious injury; there were no fractures or soft tissue damage, but it was a bad bruise and would need treatment, especially if she wanted to be ready for the Nationals.

On the Thursday before the championship weekend, Marion admitted the knee was still sore, though she insisted she would compete. "Last week, there was soreness in the knee," she said, "but I feel positive going into the meet. Hopefully, I won't have to take too many jumps."

Once again, the long jump didn't go well for Marion. The event was won by Dawn Burrell, the ninth-ranked jumper in the country. She jumped

22' 10", while the best Marion could do was a second place 22' 3". It was becoming very apparent that the long jump might well be her Achilles' heel in her quest to win five golds at the Olympics. While she was gracious in congratulating the winner, hugging Dawn Burrell, and not making any excuses, she talked later about how much losing hurt.

"Losing breaks my heart, trust me," she said. "I went back to the hotel and sulked last night. C.J. can attest to that. Losing puts things in perspective. If you win all the time, it would be easy to believe nobody could ever beat you. Losing reminds me there's going to be somebody out there who's going to pop onto the scene one day just like I did and start winning."

Coming back on Sunday, Marion defended her 200-meter championship, winning easily in 22.10. In keeping with her policy of not running too many events, she hadn't entered the 100. After the meet, a reporter asked her again about her loss in the long jump, wondering if she still felt she could go for four gold medals in the World Championships in August.

"You mean have my goals changed because I was second in the long jump?" she said. "No, they haven't. If anything, they have been put into stone."

There was another positive that came out of the meet. C. J. Hunter, whose own career had been eclipsed somewhat by Marion's, showed that he was a shot-putter to be reckoned with. He got off a great series of throws, three of them going over seventy feet, and finished second to John Godina, who was considered the best in the world. Now C.J. was also a threat in the Worlds and in the Olympics the following year.

In early August, Marion and C.J. left for Europe to get ready for the World Championships. In London on August 7, she tied her fastest time of the year in the 100, winning her race in 10.80 seconds. She finished almost three meters ahead of Shanna Pintusevich of Ukraine, who was timed in 10.98, and Inger Miller of the United States, who was third in 11.13. She remained unbeaten in track events since 1997.

"I am so far ahead of the rest of the world that everyone is just judging me by my times," Marion said. "To be frank, [the World Championships at] Seville is where it counts and there it's just about the win. The times don't matter. Obviously, the faster times will come but, at the moment, there is too much pressure on me for no reason because I'm running well."

What was the pressure? If anything, it was the constant questions about how fast she could go and her chances of beating Flo-Jo's records in the 100 and 200. It was as if people were just waiting for it to happen, and when it didn't, there was disappointment, even if her time was one of the fastest ever. It almost seemed as if everyone expected Marion to be *the* fastest. For that to happen, a whole series of circumstances would have to come together—good weather, a fast track, competition to push her, and a plain, old-fashioned great race from start to finish.

On August 11, the runners moved on to Zurich, Switzerland, where Marion entered the 200 meters. There, she held off Inger Miller to win in 22.10 seconds, her twenty-first consecutive win in that event. She seemed a lock for the 100 and 200 at the World Championships. Her relay team was also favored. The only event in question would be the long jump.

The weather in Seville was extremely hot as the athletes arrived. The events would be held at the 60,000-seat Olympic Stadium and a huge crowd was expected. But before the competition even began, there was a pall over the event. On Friday, it was announced that a 200-meter runner, Troy Douglas of the Netherlands, had failed a drug test. It was the latest in a series of similar cases involving some of the sports biggest stars. Among those suspended or fighting suspension was sprinter Merlene Ottey, high jumper Javier Sotomayor, and sprinters Linford Christie and Dennis Mitchell. Some athletes felt the testing system had to be improved. Marion, like so many others, was greatly upset about the situation.

"Over the last couple of weeks our beautiful and lovely sport has been marred by all of this," she said.

Many of the questions asked of Marion by the reporters covering the meet didn't have to do with drug testing. What seemed to be on everyone's mind was Marion's problems with the long jump. She admitted she was having problems but felt they were behind her.

"Earlier this season I was having a little difficulty with my rhythm on the runway," she said. "Since my last long jump competition we have made our necessary corrections and I feel quite confident."

In that last competition she had lost again to Heike Drechsler. However, before the championships began, word came that Drechsler had withdrawn from the competition with a calf injury. That seemed to open the door for Marion.

Former Olympic champion John Smith, who now coached men's 100-meter star Maurice Greene, was one of many in the sport anxious to see if Marion could win multiple golds. "I think it's fantastic and I can't wait to see it," Smith said. "[Marion's] going to stand on that podium four or five times. It's just a matter of which color she's going to stand there with. There's going to be some history being made and I think that the sport needs that, and [Marion] needs challenges."

As for Marion, she made no bones about the fact that she wanted four medals. When asked how she would feel if she won only three golds, she replied quickly, "I'd be disappointed, without a doubt. I mean, I'm not coming here to play games. I will be disappointed if I come back with anything less than four."

So the stage was set. The first day of the championships produced some real fireworks for both

Marion and C.J. First C.J. won the first major international championship of his career, upsetting John Godina and winning the shot put with a career best 71' 6", and doing it on his final throw of the competition. He was overjoyed.

"Other than the birth of my kids and marriage to Marion, this is the best thing in my life," the ebullient Hunter said. "I knew as soon as I let it go. I didn't want to hold back."

Asked how he and Marion would celebrate, Hunter said they would hold off any celebration until October 3, their first wedding anniversary. "Tonight we'll shake hands," C.J. said. "I'll give her a kiss, and that will be it. It's not about bragging rights. It's a family thing. She just said she was proud of me and that was it. This is the first step in fulfilling a big goal. The big picture is to do the triple—this year, next year [Olympics] and the year after [Worlds]."

The same day that C.J. got his gold, Marion took her first step, blazing down the track in 10.76 seconds to win the first heat in the 100. Her time was the fastest of the year and a record for the World Championships. "The track is fast, fast, fast," Marion said. "Watch for some world records. I'm not saying it's going to be me. Watch those men."

Then the next day, Marion won her first gold, blowing away the field in the 100-meter final and hitting the tape in 10.70 seconds, the fastest time in the world for the year and lowering the championship meet record she had set a day earlier. It was also the fifth fastest time in history. Only Marion and Flo-Jo had run faster. In the race, Marion was pushed by Inger Miller, who was second in a personal best of 10.79. It was a good win.

"I nailed my start today," Marion said. "That was perhaps the reason that I pulled off the victory. I knew Inger was running very fast, but I put it all together today and executed my race." Then, referring to her husband's victory in the shot put, Marion added, "The goal for the whole week is to get a total of five [gold medals] for the family and we've started off in wonderful fashion."

Little did Marion or C.J. know at the time, but their double-gold on the same day would end up the highlight of the championship. Within days, Marion Jones would again have her perseverance and determination tested, following a disappointment no one could have expected.

Chapter 10
Getting Back on Track

Marion's next event in the World Championships was the long jump. With Heike Drechsler out, Marion was the favorite. However, with her well-documented problems in the event, being the favorite didn't mean much. Her first jump was 22' 3¾" and left her in third place behind Fiona May and Niurka Montalvo. It wasn't looking good. It turned out to be another frustrating day in that troublesome event.

On her fourth try, Marion got off what appeared to be the best jump of the competition. The only problem was that she had fouled, starting the jump over the end of the takeoff board. More frustration. Her fifth jump of 22' 5" was her best of the series, but still left her trailing. Then, on her sixth and final try, she fouled once more. It was over. There would not be four gold medals at the World Championships as she finished third behind Montalvo and May. And the more overriding question might be; would she ever be the best in the world in this frustrating event.

"Of course, I'll be the first one to tell you my long jump needs work," she said. "My specialty is running."

Now she had to get back to running. The 200-meter dash was her next event, and absolutely no one could imagine her losing that one. The first heat on Tuesday morning showed she was in top form. She had even learned to ease up a bit toward the end, doing just enough to win and move on to the next round. But when she was getting out of the van back at her hotel after that first heat, she remarked that her back felt a little tight. "It's nothing major," she said, "but I feel it."

She had already run three heats and a final in the 100, and long jumped eight times. The track at Seville was hard and didn't have the underlayer of padding that was installed in many United States tracks. That made the track fast, but could also make it harder on the body, especially the back. When she returned to the track that evening for the second heat, the tightness was still in her back. Her massage therapist tried to loosen it, but Marion continued to feel it as she warmed up.

Then she went out and raced again, winning her heat in 22.45, once more easing up at the end. Yet forty-five minutes later, after she had cooled down and dressed, the back felt worse. In fact, she was feeling the discomfort now with just the simplest movement. She told C.J., and the medical people examined her and gave her another massage. In the morning, her back was even tighter. One of the medical people tried to place an acupuncture needle into her lower back, but the muscles were even too tight for that.

"I think I'm starting to feel spasms back there, too," she told her people. "If only I could pinpoint the area."

Her coach was working with his other athletes at the track and didn't know the full extent of the problem. When he heard what was happening, both he and Marion decided to try to get through the semifinal, then hope the forty-eight hours before the final would give her enough time to heal. She went out to the track and watched Inger Miller win the first semifinal in 22.17. Miller was improving rapidly in both the 100 and 200, giving indications that a real rivalry was developing, one that could push both runners to go even faster. Now it was Marion's turn.

She lined up in the blocks, trying not to think about the back. The huge crowd fell silent, as they always do before the start of a sprint. At the gun, Marion pushed out of the blocks. She didn't feel it was her best start, but she quickly began to stride out and challenge for the lead. As she ran into the curve, she felt it was the key to the race. If she could come off it and get onto the final straightaway, there would be no problems. But just as she finished running the curve she suddenly felt her back tightening and going into a full spasm. At first she tried to fight through it, forcing herself to pick up her knees and shift into a higher gear. It didn't work.

"I knew if I couldn't get my knees up, and if the spasming didn't stop, I was going to stop running, or I was going to take it to the ground," she would say, later, admitting, "I was so scared."

As the capacity crowd watched, Marion Jones suddenly fell to the ground, her left leg falling out to the side at an unnatural angle. She reached for her back, rolled over to the right and into the next lane, where she lay on her back with her knees in the air. It was a frightening sight and the collective gasp from the crowd confirmed it. For a minute, Marion just wanted to lay there and be left alone, hoping the pain would leave. Finally, she was put on the stretcher and taken from the track into the medical room under the stands.

With her back still spasming, Marion cried in pain and wanted only her doctors to treat her. They gave her medication to ease the pain and to control the spasms. The doctors were certain there was no disk or spinal damage, only severe muscle spasms. Finally, as she lay quietly in the room beneath the stadium, the spasms began to ease. She had to wait about two hours before she could walk. There was no way, she said, that people would see her carried out on a stretcher.

Right away there were some who felt Marion was trying to do too much, running too many races and long jumping at the same time. In meets such as the World Championships, there were simply too many heats. Couple that with the pressure, and maybe it was just too much for the body to withstand. World record holder Michael Johnson, who successfully doubled in the 200 and 400-meter runs at the 1996 Olympics, said that injuries were simply a part of the sport.

"We're athletes," Johnson said. "We get injured, especially when you're out there running as fast as Marion does. I don't think we need to second-guess her. You're hungry and you're out there to win. I applaud her for it."

The next day, agent Charlie Wells made a terse announcement. "She's out of the championships," he told the press. "She's still walking around and we're evaluating her. She still has muscle spasms in her lower back." When asked whether Marion would have to sit out the remainder of the season, Wells said, "We'll still need a couple of days to make that decision."

News of her withdrawal spread quickly and her fellow competitors quickly began to lament her loss and to sing her praises. Australian sprinter Nova Pedris-Kneebone said that Marion's absence would have a severe impact on the sport, no matter how long she was out.

"It's tragic," Pedris-Kneebone said. "In my eyes she's the Wonder Woman of track and field. She's gained so much respect."

Primo Nebiolo, president of the International Amateur Athletic Federation, said, "Marion Jones has become a symbol of all that is best in athletics, enthusiasm and the simple joy of competition."

Men's 100-meter champion Maurice Greene, who was slated to run in the men's semifinal right after Marion's race, was unnerved by her injury. "I was very nervous," he said. "My event was next. You get scared seeing an athlete go down like that. I don't think Marion was trying to do too much for her, just something she'd never tried before."

Everyone had a theory. Some felt the combination of the hard track, the very hot weather, and the rigors of the long jump all contributed to the injury. But perhaps it was arch rival Inger Miller who summed it up best. "Everyone thinks she's invincible—she's not," Miller said. "I've been telling people that."

Running in the final that Marion would miss, Inger Miller won in 21.77, which was .04 faster than Marion's best time of 1999. With the fast track and a healthy Marion, Miller might have pushed her to an even faster time. Either way, it looked as if Miller would pose a real challenge for Marion once Marion returned.

The question was when would that be? It was answered within a week. "Her season is over," Charlie Wells announced in a telephone interview from Brussels, where Marion was scheduled to compete on September 3. "She continues to improve, but she is not well enough to compete. It's unfortunate, and we know her many fans will be disappointed, but it was not worth the risk."

One of the writers noted that the decision to end Marion's season early could cost her more than one million in prize money and appearance fees. Wells added, quickly, "This is not about money. We want to look after her best welfare and the big picture."

Would the big picture still include an attempt at an unprecedented five gold medals at Sydney? Marion had done a great deal of crying in the days following her injury. But as she healed physically, she began to feel better mentally, as well. First and foremost in her mind was getting well enough to return to the track. Marion heard the stories, people saying she was doing too much, attempting too much. The old resolve began returning.

Several months after the World Championships, Inger Miller told the press she would have won the 200 even if a healthy Marion was in the race. She declared she would be very happy to spoil Marion's plans for the Olympics. "It's not just going to be the Marion Jones Show," she added.

After a more careful and detailed examination of Marion's back, doctors found a genetic condition that caused a strain on the left spinal erector. To correct the condition, doctors recommended a combination of ultrasound and exercises to strengthen her abdominal muscles, lower back, glutes, and hamstrings.

By October, Marion was given clearance to begin some light workouts. She could jog, but not run, and there was still some tight feeling in her back. She didn't push it. By November, the pain was gone. Suddenly, she could run, beginning harder workouts and tougher drills. She began to get that confident feeling that she could come all the way back. To an athlete, that's about the best feeling in the world.

Once again she heard all the reasons various people felt she had been injured. No one would ever know for sure, but she began to feel that perhaps her body was just telling her it was time for a rest. "It just happened at the worst possible time," she said.

Marion and C.J. celebrated the beginning of the new century, then continued their workouts. In late January, on a conference call with reporters, she talked about her injury and her goals.

"I don't think the long jump contributed to the back problems that occurred in Seville," Marion said. "But I realized that I have some problems with my technique. I don't have the technique down pat, but I'm willing to learn. Overall, I was pleased with the long jump at Seville. I fouled on my last attempt. I went for it. I'm proud of that. But I learned I need more competitions under my belt to gain confidence."

Marion emphasized again that she was not giving up on the long jump. In fact, she had been spending a great deal of time with that event since she resumed her training in November. She also reiterated her plans to try for five gold medals at the upcoming Olympic Games.

"After my injury in Seville, they found that the

weaknesses in my body were in my lower back, my glute, and my abdominal area. But my back has responded well to treatment and now I'm 100 percent physically."

Despite being fit again, Marion decided not to return to competition until April. That would give her time to make sure she was ready. By then, she would have been away for some eight months. Yet she was still considered the number one attraction in the sport. She signed new endorsement contracts, did more commercials, and made more personal appearances.

In mid-March, the anticipation of her return began to grow. In an interview with CNN/*Sports Illustrated*, she said again, flat out, "I'm going to Sydney entered in five events. I want to win five golds."

Marion went on to say that breaking records was not as important as winning. "If I go to Sydney and happen to run [slow] and I still win, I'll take it," she said. "The most important thing is . . . coming away with the five gold medals."

Asked if she thought she might be injury-prone, Marion dismissed the notion, saying, "I've learned to listen to my body more."

That's why she wouldn't push. She still hoped the road to Sydney would be paved with gold. Only it would be a slower road than she had taken in 1998 and 1999.

Chapter 11
Pointing Toward the Gold

Marion returned to the track on April 16, at the Mt. San Antonio College Relays in Walnut, California. The only event she entered was one she didn't really like—the 400-meter run. After a cautious start, she began to accelerate in the final turn and then left her competitors behind, winning in 49.59 seconds, which made her the fourth-fastest American woman ever at that distance. The second place finisher crossed the line in 51.16.

"I think I proved I'm back," Marion said, afterward.

Marion chose to run the 400 for a reason, saying she wanted to run a sub-50-second time and "send a message to the U.S. relay coaches [that] if they need somebody to run a 400 leg, I'm ready."

Once again, she had achieved her goal, turning in

a great time in a dramatic return. "I've had a rough time sleeping," she added, "knowing I was going to run the 400. I don't like it. I don't even like the feeling when I'm done. So I'm happy I'm finished with the 400 meters, at least until September."

As always seemed to be the case, a reporter asked about the Olympics, wondering if she might turn out to be the big story at the 2000 Games. Marion just smiled and said, "If I go to Sydney and do what I'm capable of."

To make her return an even happier occasion, C.J. showed he was ready for an Olympic run of his own. He put the shot 71 feet, 4 inches, the second-best throw of his career, and beat rival John Godina by more than 4 feet.

"I'm satisfied," C.J. said, "but I really expected to throw farther. It's the most consistent meet of my career. If I can stay consistent like this all year, it is very promising for me."

At the end of April, Marion ran in the Penn Relays, and anchored both the 400- and 800-relay teams to big wins. The meet was billed the United States vs. the World, as teams from Africa, Asia, and the Caribbean also competed. Once again, Marion was being selective about her events, getting back into competition slowly. This time she ran relays, working with the other women, getting the baton-passing techniques smoothed out, and showing everyone she still had the blazing speed.

In the 400 relay, she teamed with Chryste Gaines,

Torri Edwards, and Inger Miller to run a combined 42.33, which broke the Franklin Field and Penn Relay records. Then in the 800, running with LaTasha Jenkins, LaTasha Colander Richardson, and Nanceen Perry, the quarter broke the world record by finishing in 1 minute, 27.46 seconds.

"I was excited about running here and today did not disappoint," Marion said, "to be with two relay teams and finishing with a world record. It was sure exciting. When I got the baton [in the 800], with the crowd oohing and aahing, I wanted to bring it home."

Marion had blazed through her final 200 to ensure the record. Now that she had a 400-meter run under her belt, and had anchored two outstanding relay teams, it was time to get back to her specialties. She would run her first 100-meter race of the year at Osaka, Japan, the second week in May, and would also compete in the long jump.

"Now the season is really starting," Marion said. "The 400 really isn't my forte—it's kind of experimental—and of course, the relays are just for fun."

Then, as usual, the talk turned to the long jump. Most followers of the sport were suggesting she give up the event and concentrate on the sprints and relays, where she was rarely beaten. But she quickly indicated that quitting wasn't part of her makeup and, if anything, she had been working harder to be the best.

"I know I'm quite capable of going 7-plus meters

(22' 11¾") on Saturday," she said. "I think it will be quite evident how much more relaxed I am on the runway, just really relaxed with my approach. When I take off the board, people will quickly realize I have put in more time [training], and there will be more extension than in the past.

"It's funny," she continued, "because when I was jumping 7.31 meters [23' 11¾"] in '98 there wasn't nearly as much talk about the technique, and it was horrible. But all of a sudden in '99 when I wasn't jumping as far with the same technique, there's all these critics. So it would be really nice to go to Osaka and just really pop out a big one and kind of quiet everybody down for a little bit." The meet in Osaka had mixed results, not surprising in view of what had happened in the past. Marion won the 100 meters easily, finishing in 10.84 seconds. But once again the long jump proved frustrating. Though she fouled just once, she could not produce a big jump, nor exhibit the form that had enabled her to go over 23 feet in the past. Her best effort was 6.27 meters (20' 7") and she finished in fourth place.

"I'm disappointed," she admitted. "I felt good technique-wise in the air. I just have some adjustments to do on the runway. I've always said this would be the toughest gold to win, but I'm still going to Sydney to get five golds."

Appearing at an Olympic media summit a short time later, Marion admitted that her outspokenness about the five gold medals had opened her up for much criticism. "At times, perhaps, I wish I would have left it as a surprise," she said, "maybe kept it quiet a little longer. Then maybe I wouldn't be getting some of the criticism I get. If something happens and I don't win all five, I'll have to cope with that. I'm going to go there and try to win everything I possibly can win."

Marion continued to work into the summer. As one of the highest-profile track stars in the country, she also spoke out about issues other than the medals she hoped to win in Sydney. She often talked about athletes being positive role models, equal pay for women athletes, and the importance of athletes getting their college degrees, even if they turn pro early. To emphasize the points she wanted to make, Nike put her in a series of television ads that showed only the lower half of her face as she spoke into a microphone. Each ad ended with her saying the words, "Can you dig it?"

"The feedback I have received has been so positive," she said. "The purpose of the ads was to get some of these messages out that people sometimes don't hear me talk about. I'd say eighty-five percent of the people who came up to me said something about the commercials, or said something about 'go get it.' I was so impressed that people in the general public were realizing it was me."

So it continued into the summer. There were no questions about Marion's running. She seemed to be all the way back, once again appearing unbeatable in the 100 and 200. The x-factor remained the long jump, with everyone wondering if Marion could ever regain her success of 1998 when she was the number one ranked long jumper in the world. Her coach, Trevor Graham, seemed willing to try anything at this point. He told the media that any efforts to learn a new technique were being abandoned and that Marion was returning to her 1998 style of speed-jumping.

"I've told her to just run down the runway, use her speed, hang [in the air] and jump as far as she can," Graham said.

Her first time going back to speed-jumping didn't produce the expected results. At the Pontiac Grand Prix Invitational meet on June 17, Marion was beaten in the long jump by her training partner, Chandra Sturrup of Bahama. Sturrup jumped 21' 11¾", while Marion was second with a leap of 21' 6". Would it ever get better? The only good news from the meet was C.J. winning the shot put, with a world best throw of 71' 8¾". Once again Marion had mixed feelings.

"Anytime I compete, I love to win," she said. "I thrive on it. When I don't win I'm a little sour. As for C.J., I know he is the best in the world. You [reporters] are the ones who seem surprised, not us."

In the final week of June, there was a ray of hope. Competing in the Prefontaine Classic Grand Prix meet in Eugene, Oregon, Marion got a double. Wearing a flashy new full bodysuit designed by

Nike, she won the 100 in a wind-aided 10.93. More importantly, she then won the long jump with a leap of 22' 10½", her best effort of the year and perhaps a sign that she was ready to make a return to her top form, something that would give her a chance to get the one gold that so many people doubted she could win.

In the meantime, she and C.J. are featured in another commercial that shows them frolicking in a supermarket. C.J. is shot-putting grapefruits, and Marion is speeding around the store catching them. It's a fun spot, showing two world-class athletes who happen to be husband and wife, having some fun while publicizing their sport.

Will Marion Jones make track history at the 2000 Olympics? That certainly seems to be the main theme as the Games come closer and the excitement builds. Dick Ebersole, the president of NBC, the television network that will cover the Games, has already stated publicly that the network will cover Marion's attempt to win the unprecedented five gold medals "like a miniseries." And, as one major sports magazine said in early July, "Perhaps no female athlete in history has been more aggressively marketed than the expected star of the 2000 Games."

That expected star, of course, is Marion Jones. Her quest began at the Olympic Trials, which were held in Sacramento, California, in July. The biggest question was answered when she won the long jump competition to assure herself a chance to win five golds. Next come the Games in September. The International Olympic Committee has already arranged the schedule so that it will be possible for her to achieve her dream. But it will be a physically grueling schedule and Marion will have to perform flawlessly to win. This is what she will have to do and when she will have to do it.

- Friday, September 22—Some time after 1:05 P.M., Australian time, Marion will run in one of the seven heats in the first round of the 100 meters. Later that day, after 8:15 P.M., she will run in one of the four heats in the second round of the 100.
- Saturday, September 23—Around 6:30 P.M., she will run in the semifinals of the 100 meters. At 8:05 P.M., she will run in the 100-meter finals.
- Sunday, September 24 through Tuesday, September 26—Marion will have these days to rest.
- Wednesday, September 27—After 11:15 A.M., she will run in one of the six heats of the first round of the 200-meter dash. After 6:55 P.M., she will run in one of the four heats in the second round of the 200. Then, after 8:05 P.M., she will compete in the qualifying round of the long jump.
- Thursday, September 28—At 6:00 P.M., she will run in the 200-meter semifinals. At 7:55 P.M., she will race in the 200-meter finals.

• Friday, September 29—After 10:45 A.M., she will compete in one of the four heats in the first round of the 4 x 100-meter relays. After 6:40 P.M., she will run in one of the three heats in the first round of the 4 x 400-meter relays. At 7:20 P.M., the competition for the long jump finals will begin. Then, at 8:20 P.M., she will run in the 4 x 100-meter relay semi-finals.

• Saturday, September 30—At 7:40 P.M., Marion will run in the 4 x 100-meter relay final. She will finish up at 9:35 P.M. when she will run in the 4 x 400-meter relay final.

If she can complete this rigorous schedule in top form, with no unexpected setbacks, and compete at the top of her form, she can win the five gold medals she so covets. If she does it, she will have done something considered incredibly special. She will also become a real American star, an athlete who could transcend her sport as only a few, special people such as Michael Jordan, Muhammad Ali, and Tiger Woods have done. She can also play a huge role in putting track and field back on the map as an exciting American sport for everyone.

Of course, if something happens and she doesn't make it, she shouldn't be criticized. For Marion Jones has the courage not to fear failure. She has set her goals high, as she has since she was a young girl, and has never wavered. Whether it was basketball or track, Marion has been a leader, a doer, an achiever, and a winner. She has overcome a series of obstacles and setbacks, personal çonflicts and injuries, and has always reemerged on top. Come September, the world will be focused upon her as she tries to make a dream come true and as the best athletes in the entire world try to stop her. Win or lose, it should make for heart-stopping drama.

Can you dig it?

About the Author

Bill Gutman has been a freelance writer for more than twenty years. In that time he has written many books for children and adults, a lot of which are about sports. He has written profiles and biographies of many sports stars from both past and present, and some lesser ones as well. Aside from biographies, his sports books include histories, how-to instructionals, and sports fiction. He is the author of Archway's *Sports Illustrated* series, biographies of Bo Jackson, Michael Jordan, Shaquille O'Neal, Grant Hill, Tiger Woods, Ken Griffey, Jr., Brett Favre, and Sammy Sosa; and *NBA High-Flyers*, profiles of top NBA stars. All are available from Archway Paperbacks. Mr. Gutman currently lives in Dover Plains, New York, with his wife and family.

Don't Miss a Single Play!

Archway Paperbacks Brings You the Greatest
Games, Teams, and Players in Sports!

By

Bill Gutman

☆Football Super Teams

☆Bo Jackson: A Biography

☆Michael Jordan: A Biography (revised)

☆Baseball Super Teams

☆Great Quarterbacks of the NFL

☆Tiger Woods: A Biography

☆ Ken Griffey, Jr.: A Biography

☆ Brett Favre: A Biography

☆Sammy Sosa: A Biography

☆Shaquille O'Neal: A Biography (revised)

 An Archway Paperback
Published by Pocket Books

630-13

WNBA

STARS OF WOMEN'S BASKETBALL

Take to the courts with league MVP Cynthia Cooper. Go eye to eye with unblinking Sheryl Swoopes. Pound the boards with superstar and supermodel Lisa Leslie. And see what's *really* happening in the red-hot game of women's basketball! Here's everything you need to know about the teams—and the players—that are putting the bad-boy superstars of the NBA in their place. Packed with photos, stats, profiles, interviews, team spotlights, and Q&As, this slam-dunking book tells the amazing stories behind these phenomenal players.

by James Ponti

Now available!

 An Archway Paperback
Published by Pocket Books